I0542384

TO STAND CLOSE

FAITH ASHLIN

TO STAND CLOSE

Dedication

For my big sister, K. I'll love you always.

Chapter One

With her face creased in concentration, the young gymnast landed well from the mid-air somersaults, her feet making solid contact with the mat. But rather than creating an elaborate show of her stability, she immediately arched backward, stretching her spine into a perfect curve. Her arm came up above her head, elbow soft, hand following the movement, as she looked backward along the line, making sure every finger was in the right place, delicate and gentle.

The extra gesture followed perfectly with the music, a quiet, haunting piece of heartbreaking intensity with only a single clear voice laid over the melody. She followed the sound with her hand, her arm, her whole body, faced creased with the feeling of the music, till the very last note.

Then she was still. Perfectly, completely still, caught in the moment and the magic. For a long second she kept the position, fixed in time, then the spell was broken as she turned toward her coach, a sixteen-year-old girl once more. "Nicky?" she asked, her attention fixed on his face. "Was it good enough?"

Nicky took a slow breath as he pulled himself up from where he sat, just outside the floor area. "How did it feel to you?"

"It felt..." Adeline caught her lip between her teeth, uncertainty seeming to creep over her like a plague as she dipped her head, suddenly aware of everyone else in the gym.

"No." He stopped her. "Doesn't matter how anyone else reacts. How did it feel to you?"

Her focus was back on him again, as though he were the only important thing in the world. The only thing. "Like I'd become part of the music. L—like I could feel it in my tummy, like I was in it. It felt... I felt..." She stopped, shaking her head.

"Beautiful," he said quietly. "You looked beautiful. You were beautiful. Beautiful—that's the word you want. You and the music were beautiful."

She stared at him, her heart and soul in her eyes, all being offered to him, then she broke into a huge grin. "And the triple twist somersault?"

"Over cooked and off line." He shrugged, grinning back. "But we can sort that out later. It doesn't matter—you caught the essence, the soul of it. Who cares about a bit of a wobble when you're that graceful?"

"The judges will, you idiot." She laughed, running toward him. "That would be at least a point two deduction."

"And another point two off your score for not being straight." He slung an arm over her shoulder, leading her across the hall. "But I'd give you an extra couple of marks for taking my breath away."

"Idiot," she repeated, smiling and leaning into him for a moment. Her hand went up toward his face, hovering for a moment near the birthmark covering his cheek on one side. She gave it the briefest of touches with one fingertip, then she ran away as he pushed her gently.

"Okay, everyone, warm down then home. I, for one, need some sleep."

There was a chorus of cheeky replies and a few harmless insults before the group of girls got together on the floor area to go through their ritual warm down. Nicky started clearing up—a water bottle here, a track suit top there, putting mats back in their proper place—as he listened to them.

They were still laughing and giggling together—amazing after a three-hour, strenuous work out. Comments about their haircuts mixed in with gossip from favorite TV shows and the latest pop star as they took care of muscles that had been worked hard. Nicky stopped and watched them, a collection of hand guards held against his chest. They were damned good girls. Not just at gymnastics—that went without saying. But a collection of diverse personalities that had one thing in common—they were all good people. Some were loud and confident, others softly spoken or wary, but they would all grow up to be decent adults.

He had chosen the group well. Not just great gymnasts—not even always the best he had seen, there had been other, better, gymnasts he had turned down—but great gymnasts with better characters who he could work with. Who he could help become the best in the world. He smiled at them fondly.

"What are you staring at, old man?" Martha stood, hands on hips, and pulled a face at him, sticking out her tongue.

"A stick insect with red hair?"

"A stick insect?" She narrowed her eyes. "If I'm such a stick insect, why did you have that soppy expression your face? You looked a sausage short of a barbeque."

He barked out a laugh at the absurdity of her comparison and knew that the soppy expression was back again. "Because I'm proud of you," he said seriously. "I'm proud of all of you."

Martha stopped for a moment, her face showing her pride in the compliment, then she was off again, running toward the showers. "I told you he's gone soft in the head," she shouted over her shoulder to the others. "It's because he doesn't spend enough time having fun."

"If I have gone soft, it's because I spend too much time with you guys." He threw a hand guard half-heartedly after her, knowing he'd have to pick it up himself, and shook his head. He was proud of them, each and every one. "And why are you all in such a rush to get out of here?"

"Because" — Martha popped her head back round the changing room door — "as we did so well in the last competition, our mums have given us money to go late night shopping. We're buying something other than leotards and track suits for once, something glamorous. High heels and skirts with spangles on them." She grinned again, flashing her teeth. "Unlike you, we know how to have fun."

"So, go, have fun." He waved them away. "Just don't be late for training in the morning." He picked up the hand guard and looked round the gym. All ready for the next day. He collected his things and reached for the light switch, muttering to himself, "I do know how to have fun, if I remember right."

Outside in the corridor he held the main door open for the last of his girls as they headed off, still talking a mile a minute. But before he could lock up, one of the girls' mothers stopped him, her foot in the door, her hand pressed against his chest.

Mrs. Bygroves. She'd always made him want to take a step away. Too pushy, too knowing, too self-assured. "Nicky." She purred his name. "We wanted to have a quick word with you."

"We?"

"Myself and the other mothers." She indicated the group of women behind her, already starting to move toward the door. "We won't keep you long. We just wanted to give you something to say a proper thank you for all you've done for our girls, especially after the amazing results at the last competition."

"You don't have to give me anything." He hesitated, already not liking the feel of this. "I do it for the pleasure of working with them, and they've already said thank you."

"Nonsense." She pushed past him, confidently making her way to the office. "I know the authorities don't recognize your work as they should and I'll wager they never say thank you."

"It doesn't matter." He trailed after the women. What else could he do?

"But you're the best women's gymnastics coach in the country. You should be working with the elite national squad, not stuck out here in the middle of nowhere."

"But I'm building a better squad than the national elite one." He allowed himself a satisfied smile. Yeah, his girls were damned good.

"And that should be recognized," Mrs. Milton said, smiling. "What you've done for my Carrie is amazing. We all appreciate it."

"Well, thank you," he said, following them all into the office to stand awkwardly in the middle of the circle they made around him. He folded his arms over his chest then deliberately made himself lower them. He never did know how to behave around people like this. They made him feel awkward and out of his depth. "But you don't have to give me anything. That really isn't necessary."

"Nonsense," Mrs. Bygroves took over again. "You're going to love your present and I'm sure we will as well. It's only fair you get a reward, and if it can't be national recognition, then I'm sure this will make up for it." She grinned — a knowing, almost sly sort of grin. "Will you bring it in, please," she asked a couple of the other women. They left after giving equally knowing looks and there was another uncomfortable moment when they all stood and stared at each other.

"Here it is," Mrs. Bygroves said at last, as there came a noise behind Nicky from the doorway. The attention of all the women facing him was fixed on the scene behind him and he turned slowly to see what held their attention so firmly.

Standing just inside the room was a very tall, very naked man with shaggy hair, a blank face and the most closed off eyes Nicky had ever seen. His hands hung limply by his side and there on his chest and calf were his slave serial numbers.

Nicky took a defensive step backwards, his mouth dry, his mind screaming at him to get out of there. "What...?" But he didn't want to think about the rest of the question, didn't want to know. Only there was no way the indomitable Mrs. Bygroves was going to allow him the luxury of ignorance, even if he was only fooling himself.

"We've bought you your very own sex slave. Isn't that wonderful?"

Nicky's face froze in horror, and he took another step away.

"We all know what a...quiet little life you lead. It's all work, work, work, which is great for our girls but everyone should have some fun. Don't you think so? Yes, of course you do." She answered her own question and went on without taking a breath. "So we thought this would be an excellent idea. You get all the fun you can handle." At that point she actually nudged his shoulder. "But there's no effort required. You can do what you like, when the need is there, without explanations, or the necessity of dinners out or even conversation. Just think of it, Nicky. Whatever, whenever, with no questions or repercussions. Doesn't that sound perfect?"

"No." Nicky suddenly found his voice. "No, no, no. I don't want a slave. I really don't want anything to do with him and..."

"You don't like our present?" Mrs. Milton said, her voice was very controlled, very tight. Nicky heard the tone all too clearly. Mrs. Bygroves might be too self-assured for his liking but Mrs. Milton was the one who worked in the government. Worked at too a high a level for anyone to ask her exactly what she did.

"I didn't mean it like that," he backtracked. "Thank you for the present. It was really kind of you to think of me, but I don't need anything. It's privilege enough to work with the girls. As for...him." He waved his hand in the general direction of the slave. "I have no time for him. I can't manage..."

"Nonsense," Mrs. Bygroves pushed in again. "We all know what men are like. We're sure you'll make time for him." Several laughed in a significant way, too high-pitched and laced with something sour. "I mean, just look at him." And they all did, their gaze running over oceans of naked flesh as the slave just stood there, not reacting at all. "Of course you want him."

"No." Nicky had to stand firm, this was so very wrong. "It's a lovely gesture, but I have to say no. I can't have a slave. I just can't."

There was a soft touch to his arm and Sue Westwell, Adeline's mousy, widowed mother, peered up at him, her eyes full of concern. "You really don't want him?" she asked softly.

"No, I don't."

"So what do you expect us to do with him?" Mrs. Bygroves said, her mouth puckered with disapproval. "We all clubbed together, and he's already paid for."

"Can't you sell him and get your money back?" Nicky's attention went from her to the slave. The very naked slave. "It was good of you all but..."

"You want us to take him back to the slave market?" she asked. And if Nicky hadn't been looking, he would never have seen the shadow of pure fear that suddenly filled the slave's eyes. "We can't—we registered him in your name. He's officially your slave, so if you want to sell him, you'll have to go take him to the market."

Again the flash of fear in the slave's eyes, but this time it was matched by something in Nicky's belly. He'd heard about the slave market—'the meat market' as it was commonly known—had heard tales of what went on there. He'd never been, and he never wanted that situation to change.

But he didn't want a slave, couldn't possibly have one.

Perhaps he could get someone to take the slave for him. He'd have to pay of course, and that would be a problem but...his mind raced with possibilities. Then he'd have to give the mothers their money back and... He didn't mean to, but he couldn't help glancing back at the slave.

The man's head had dropped a little, and now he stared at the bottom of the wall opposite. But the deep breaths he was taking were clearly evident from the rise and fall of his chest, and his fingers had curled into his palms. The fear in his eyes hadn't faded from the second mention of the slave market. Hadn't faded in the least.

If you bothered to look.

I don't want a slave, can't possibly have one.

"So what are you going to do?" Mrs. Bygroves's earlier excitement had gone. Now there was a discontented tightening to her face. She always did like things to go the way she planned. "Are you throwing our present back at us?" she snorted. "It's your loss. I suppose we could take him back to the market now. If I come with you, you can give me the money right away. I'll make sure everyone gets their share."

The slave held his breath.

Nicky's hands curled into fists. Fight or flight? Flight seemed like a great option right then.

I don't want a slave, can't possibly have one.

"Come on then," she said, disapproval thick in her voice. "I should have known better, seeing as it's you. Let's get this over with. We'll go in my car, of course."

I don't want a slave, can't possibly have one.

The slave's lips pressed so hard together that the blood disappeared from them, leaving them the same color as his ashen face.

"No," Nicky said, although he would have sworn he never made the decision to do so. His shoulders drooped as any fight left him, and he bowed to the inevitable. "I'll keep him."

"You will?" Sue Westwell asked uncertainly. "Are you sure?"

"Of course he's sure." Mrs. Bygroves laughed. "Just look at what we've given him." Then all eyes were back on the slave who stood impassively once more. "Who the hell would turn that down?" she added, wistfully.

I would, Nicky thought. *I would in a heartbeat...if I hadn't seen that flicker in his eyes.* But that option had been taken away from him, and now he was stuck.

"Well," Mrs. Bygroves went on. "I suppose we should leave these two to get better acquainted." She nudged his shoulder again. "I can imagine what fun you're going to have tonight, you lucky thing. Come on ladies, we need to leave Nicky alone with his thank you present." She began to usher the others out.

Sue Westwell paused as she passed. "I do hope we did the right thing. Everyone said, but...I do hope it was right." She gave a weak smile and was gone.

Mrs. Milton hung back, collecting up some things before turning to Nicky. "You should have this." She dumped a holdall into his arms. "It's the slave's clothes and stuff, although I can't imagine you'll have much need for clothes. Oh, and these." She added a thick, large envelope on the top. "Those are his papers. He's all legal and registered to you, everything is above board." Then she followed the others out.

Mrs. Bygroves was the last to leave. "Anything you want," she whispered close to his ear. "Just think of it, anything you want at any time, with no consequences." Then she too was gone, leaving just Nicky and a very naked slave.

His own very naked slave.

"Fuck, shit, balls..." Nicky couldn't think of any worse words. He wanted to go home, sit on his sofa in his ratty old bathrobe and do nothing, think of nothing. Instead he had a slave to deal with. A naked slave. "Fuck, fuck, fucking..." What else was there to say? He heaved in a huge breath, held it till he could feel the blood pounding in his temple, the air straining his lungs, then let it go in a rush.

He looked down at the things in his arms — it was easier than looking at the slave. "You have clothes in here?" He held out the bag but the slave didn't react. "If you do, put some on. I can't think...I'm not... Shit. Fucking assholes." He huffed again before dropping the bag on the floor and pushing it over to the slave with his foot.

"I'm just going to...to do something, somewhere outside in the corridor while you get dressed. Then we can... Fucking, shit, fuck." He did his damnedest not to storm out but to appear as if he was in some kind of control. He wasn't sure that banging the door closed was quite the effect he wanted.

He leaned back against the wall next to the door, rubbed at his closed eyes, exhaling hard yet again, and cursed the fact he didn't smoke. He didn't know what to do, what to think, what to say to the slave. A cigarette might have helped. He wished Beth, his assistant coach, had been at work today. She always knew what to do and if nothing else, she might have been able to head off the mums.

She might have been able to get him out of this.

But she wasn't here, and there was nothing else for it but to get on and deal with the slave inside. The hopefully no longer naked slave.

He huffed once more, just for the sake of it, pulled himself off the wall, squared his shoulders, tucked the envelope under his arm and opened the door. A tiny bit of his luck had held – the slave was wearing baggy, torn jeans, a pair of scuffed trainers and the black T-shirt with a big red circle on it that slaves were required to wear at all time.

It wasn't perfect but it was a start.

"I guess we'd better go?" Nicky didn't really mean it as a question but he couldn't help how it came out. He tried again. "Let's go."

The slave glanced at him then down at the bag without saying anything. "Yes." Nicky didn't know if he was agreeing or asking or what. "Bring that with you. My car is outside, we should get going and…" And what was he meant to say? He led the way out, turning off lights and locking the main doors behind him.

"Over here." He pointed at the small, old car with the dent in the side that he really did mean to fix one of these days. It was almost at the top of his 'to do' list. Right after 'figure out what the fuck to do with a slave you don't want.' The slave shuffled to a stop beside him and stood very still. "I know it's old and crappy but it still works – most of the time – and that's what counts, right? As long as it gets from A to B and it doesn't rain too much, because the water has a habit of getting in, and the wipers don't work too well, that's if they work at all, but…"

Why was he apologizing to a slave for the state of his car? That wasn't how things worked, not in this country. Slaves were for using and fucking – nothing else. And that was pretty much why Nicky didn't even want to know about them. He pursed his lips and unlocked the car door before going round to the driver's side to unlock that. Central locking? In his dreams.

The slave carefully slid his way in, still clutching the holdall to his chest, and Nicky started the car.

"Put your seatbelt on. Last thing I need is getting stopped by the police. If they look at the tires on this thing I'm in deep shit."

It wasn't till he was nearly home that he realized the whole journey had been spent with him talking crap and the slave not saying a word. But he might as well wait till they got inside now. "It's just over there," he said, nodding with his chin. "The top of that little building sandwiched between the defunct bowling alley and the laundry. The laundry is always open but it's weird, you never see anyone going in or out. Perhaps it's all done by machine or Oompa Loompas. I don't know." He had to stop talking. Had to.

He drove round the back, trying to avoid the potholes, parked close up to the fence and waited for the car to give its last shudder after he switched it off. The silence was thick, almost palpable in the small space, like a living thing bearing down on him. The presence of the other man, the heat coming from his body, the shallow sound of his breaths, the sheer physical size of him, pressed into Nicky.

"Shall we go in?" he asked, although he knew it was stupid. He was the owner, not the slave. "It's up the top. I'll just knock on Miss Forbat's door. She lives downstairs. She's about a million years old and hardly ever goes out, but she notices everything that goes on and…" He willed himself to stop talking and got out of the car.

The slave followed him very slowly and Nicky waited patiently before locking the car. "This way." He tapped lightly on a door that was tucked next to a steep staircase. The curtain of the window next to it pulled back before it was opened, and a tiny wizened face, with knot of wispy gray hair on top and bright red lipstick, poked out.

"Hi, Miss F." Nicky smiled. "How you doing?"

"Fine," she said, same as she always did, which made Nicky smile. Same as he always did. "Are you home for the night?"

"Yes, ma'am. Tell me in the morning if you need me to pick anything up on the way home or..." Nicky came to a stop as he realized she wasn't listening. She was too busy looking round him at the slave. "This is..." He didn't know who it was. "He's..." What was he meant to say? She could see he was a slave by his clothes, but Nicky didn't want to explain everything. Not right then. "He's staying with me."

"Staying with you? You never have anyone stay except that Beth, when she's too drunk to get back to her own home. A nice girl. Shame you're not that way inclined."

Nicky didn't want to have that conversation yet again. "Yeah, well, he's staying with me for..." How long for? "A while."

"How long's 'a while'?" she asked but Nicky had had enough. He made a break for the stairs.

"Night, Miss F. Sleep well."

At the top he opened his door and stood back waiting for the slave to go in, but he wasn't there. No slave would run, not in this country. No matter how bad things were, none would be stupid enough to run, the consequences were simply too awful. He glanced back—the slave was still making his slow way up the stairs. "Are you all right?" he asked, and the slave gave the briefest of nods.

Nicky waited for him, watching. He was walking, moving carefully, holding himself tight, each step precise and planned. "Are you really all right?" He asked again as the slave passed him.

Again the brief nod.

"You don't say much, do you?" Nicky ushered him through the door directly into the small kitchen and locked the door behind them. "In fact, you don't say anything at all." He dropped his keys on the counter as the slave stood impassively. "Can you talk?"

Again a nod.

"But you're not going to?"

This time the very tip of the slave's tongue wiped over his bottom lip in a tiny, hardly there gesture. But Nicky kept his mouth shut for once, waiting. After a long, long pause the slave took a small breath. "Told not to."

"Told by who?"

Another small lick of his lips. "At the Slave Preparation Center."

"Oh." Nicky caught his breath. He'd heard about those places, nasty stories told by those who'd drunk enough to loosen their tongues. Vile stories of things he didn't want to think about. It was Nicky's turn to lick at his lips. "Are you all right?"

This time the slave went back to a single, quick nod.

"No," Nicky said quickly, his mind whirring through a thousand possibilities. He'd seen the slave naked, there hadn't appeared to be a mark on him. But Nicky had heard the stories, knew what could be done without leaving visible evidence. "I'm telling you that you can talk, I want you to. Talk to me, tell me, are you okay?"

"I will be," the slave said softly.

"Do you need a doctor?"

The slave's eyes didn't meet Nicky's but he did lift his head. "The doctor was as bad. Nearly."

"Oh," Nicky said again. Yeah, he'd heard all slaves had a medical examination before they were sold, to check for everything. "Do you need a regular doctor? I have one I could call."

"No." The slave shook his head, still hanging onto the bag for dear life.

Nicky didn't know what to do next. "Can I get you something? Is there anything you need?"

The slave stood silently.

"Are you hungry?" At that the slave's head shot up and he even peeped in Nicky's direction as he nodded. "Come on," Nicky said. "Talk to me."

The slave's fingers tightened on the bag. "Yes, I'm hungry."

This Nicky could handle. "Okay then, you sit down and I'll see what I have. What do you like?"

"Anything," the slave said quickly and with feeling he didn't appear to be able to control.

"Right. Even I can do anything." Nicky opened the fridge door knowing there wasn't much inside. But maybe he'd forgotten something. "Eggs?" he asked without turning round. "There are a few of them left, and I know I have bread. How about scrambled eggs on toast? Will that do?"

Now he did turn, and the slave was still standing exactly where he had been.

"It's okay," Nicky said softly. "Sit down, put the bag down. Unless you don't want scrambled eggs on toast?"

The slave seemed to react as though it were a threat—if he didn't sit, he didn't get fed. Nicky was acutely reminded of the few times he'd been really hungry. But he'd never been as hungry as the slave seemed. "Are you okay to sit there while I cook?"

Nicky made sure his tone was gentle, no hint of anything nasty in it.

The slave nodded.

"Right." Nicky steadied himself, glancing round his tiny kitchen area. He grabbed a pan and a bowl then cracked eggs while simultaneously putting bread into the toaster. As he stirred the mixture in the pan, the room filled with the smell of the food. He wasn't a great cook but even he had to admit it was a comforting smell. When he glanced over, just about to comment as much, the slave was staring at the warm toast intently, his mouth pinched tight.

Quickly Nicky buttered the bread and pushed the plate across the table. "Here, you start on this while I finish the other stuff."

For the first time the slave looked him straight in the face, hesitation and need warring in his eyes.

"Go on," Nicky urged him, then turned away deliberately. It was silent for a long moment then there was the sound of the slave pouncing on the food and eating it with indigestion inducing speed. Nicky loaded the toaster again.

A wave of nausea suddenly hit him as he realized that this wasn't allowed. The government would most certainly not approve of what he was doing. The slave was sitting at the table, while his owner cooked for him. No, there was no way that would be allowed. He could beat, rape and even kill his slave, but not do something for him. If some nosey-parker saw this and decided to report them... He pulled down the blind at the small window and went back to cooking.

When he'd filled the two plates, he put them on the table, along with mugs of coffee, and sat opposite the slave. The table was so small that the edges of their plates almost touched and their knees would have knocked underneath, if the slave hadn't made way for Nicky. This time the slave didn't start eating until Nicky did, and stopped when he did, so Nicky was careful to keep up a slow but continuous momentum.

He also watched the slave while trying not to be too obvious about it. The man was clearly extremely hungry but—like with any harm that had been done to him at the Slave Preparation Center—there was nothing noticeable. He didn't seem emaciated or gaunt, but the way he pulled the plate as close as possible to him, one arm curved around it as he wolfed down his food, spoke volumes.

"So," Nicky said for lack of anything else to start with. "What do I call you?"

The slave stopped eating, the fork half way to his mouth. He inhaled, dropped his eyes, put the food back on the plate and said very flatly and carefully, "Whatever you want."

"Whatever I want? What does that mean?" Nicky asked, sharper than he meant.

"Most owners just call us 'slave', but if there's another name you like..." He left the implication hanging but it was still more than he'd said since Nicky had first seen him. Nicky was surprised when the slave went on. "And they said I call you master."

"No you don't," Nicky said, vehemently. "No way. My name is Nicky, so call me that. What's your name?"

"Whatever you..."

"No," Nicky interrupted, then made a conscious effort to soften his tone. "What's your name?"

The slave lifted his head and looked at Nicky for the second time. "Michael," he said simply.

"Hi, Michael." Nicky reached across the table, offering his hand.

It was a long moment before Michael wiped his palm on his thigh and hesitantly shook it. "Hi," he said quietly.

"Now, eat," Nicky instructed, "before it gets cold. In fact..." He emptied the rest of his food onto Michael's plate. "Have this as well, I've had enough." Again Michael looked at him sharply. "Go on, I had cakes earlier. One of the girls made them for me, to say thank you for helping them through the competition. It was a damned sight better present than the one their mothers gave me."

Michael went still.

"No, I didn't mean it like that. It's just that I...fuck. How am I meant to explain this?" He got up and found the half empty bottle of whiskey at the back of the cupboard and automatically poured out two glasses, setting one in front of Michael. "It's not you, I have nothing against you. It's just that I didn't—don't—want a slave. I'm just an ordinary guy. People like me don't have slaves. I live in this tiny place, I work and that's it, that's my life. There's no place in it for a slave, but it's not about you."

Michael had finished most of the food in record time but now paused, his hand on the full glass of whiskey.

"You can talk to me," Nicky said. But he could guess what the slave had been told, made to believe. "In fact, I'm telling you to talk to me." He could see the effort it took for Michael to glance up at him.

"Are you taking me back to the market?" Every muscle in Michael's body was held tight, clamped down and controlled by sheer will. No one should have to do that.

"No." Nicky sighed, slumping back into his chair. "Maybe I could have if I hadn't brought you here but not now. Your name's Michael, you're hungry and they've scared the ever-living shit out of you. You're a person, not a slave. No, I can't take you back there." He snorted to himself, shaking his head. "I have no fucking idea what I am going to do but don't worry, you're safe here. And..." He slapped his hand down on the table, making sure he had Michael's attention. "While I'm around, you're safe and I'm not going to let anyone else near you. Okay?"

Michael stared at him but didn't move.

"Okay?" Nicky repeated.

"Okay," Michael said.

"Good." Nicky knocked his glass against Michael's. "Let's drink on it." It only took a moment for Michael to copy him, knocking back the pale liquid. "So tonight we'll just not think about how I'm going to handle things and forget about the rest of the world and..." Michael was scraping up every last morsel of food from his plate, almost wiping it clean.

Nicky got up, trying to carry on the flow of conversation as he found more food. "Do you want a bath or a shower after we've eaten?" He put a half-eaten packet of biscuits on the table and a couple of bananas, nodding to them when Michael didn't move. "The hot water heater should have switched on an hour ago so there'll be enough. Yeah?"

After finishing his first biscuit, Michael cleared his throat. "A bath would be good, if you don't mind."

"No, sure, if that's what you want. Eat first then help yourself." He paused for a moment, considering. "Your accent, you're not from here, are you?"

"No. Not from anywhere like here."

"I thought not. I've haven't heard anything like it, except on the TV and..." Nicky stopped, watching as Michael started on a banana, his movements still contained and controlled, his body held tight. This time Nicky went to the top cupboard, searching around on the shelf. "These are the strongest painkillers I have," he said gently. "I got them when I hurt my back last year, they're good. Take as many as you need." He set the packet down next to Michael's hand.

"Thank you," Michael said softly, already swallowing two with the last of his coffee.

"And eat the rest of the food. There's no reason not to."

Michael reached for the last of the biscuits.

"Shall I make you a sandwich? More toast?"

"No." Michael shook his head. "This is enough." He indicated the last remaining banana. "Thank you."

"You sure?"

This time Michael nodded. "Shouldn't eat too much. Not at first."

"Not after going without."

Michael tipped his head but didn't say anything.

"Okay. Come on, I'll give you the grand tour. It should last all of twenty seconds." He got up and Michael followed, bringing the fruit with him. "This, obviously, is the pathetic excuse for a kitchen." He led the way out into a hall that was no more than five meters long. "That's the bathroom." He pushed back the door showing an old-fashioned bathroom suite complete with shower over the tub and a plastic curtain.

"The bedroom is large enough for a bed, wardrobe, one cupboard and no room to stand up." Again he pushed open the door. "And last but not least, the living room." Behind this door there was a shabby green two-seater sofa with sagging but comfortable cushions, an armchair that didn't match, a tiny coffee table and a small, out-of-date TV with a video tape player. Every other available surface was covered in piles of tapes and books—hundreds and hundreds of books stacked on the floor, the chairs and the flimsy looking shelves. "The TV works, most of the time. But don't count on it." He shrugged absently. "I don't always notice. I read a lot. Anyway that's it, my home." He turned to see Michael watching him. "But you're safe here, and no one can make you leave but me. You're safe."

"Thank you," Michael said, a little more confidently than before.

"Bath now?"

"Please." Michael nodded.

"You run the water, I'll find a towel."

When Michael was settled, Nicky pulled the bathroom door closed as far as its rusty hinges would allow and went back to the kitchen. He got out his phone as he started to clear up, calling Beth, his assistant coach and best friend. He tried to keep his voice low as he explained to her what had happened, knowing that Michael would be able to hear his furtive whispers in the bathroom. Nothing he could do about that when none of the doors closed properly.

He had turned off the lights, locked up and was in the bedroom when Michael came out, a towel wrapped around his waist. "Okay?" Nicky asked.

Michael nodded then seemed to think better of it. "The pills helped, I feel better," he volunteered.

"Good." Nicky had already changed into the old T-shirt he wore for bed and slipped off his jogging bottoms before squeezing past to get to the bathroom. "Help yourself to anything else you want."

When he got back, Michael was still standing where he'd left him, still in the towel. "I put your bag over there," he said softly. "But you only have slave T-shirts and sweatshirts, right?"

"Yes, it's all we're allowed to wear."

"But no one can see in here and it's no one's business but ours, so I thought you might prefer to wear this." Nicky handed him an old T-shirt of his own. Michael stared at it, then him, confused. "I mean you can't wear it out or in the day when someone might see, but I figured it must be nicer to wear it at night," Nicky went on.

Michael licked at his lip. "You want me to wear it when we have…or do you mean when I sleep?"

"When we have what?" Nicky dug clean clothes out of the drawer, ready for the morning.

"Sex," Michael said, levelly.

"Whoa." Nicky stopped, turning to look straight at Michael. "I don't want sex with you. I don't want a slave, and I don't want sex. I can do casual — although I don't even do much of that — but I can't handle non-consensual. Forget that idea, there's not going to be any sex."

"But that's what I'm for. Why they bought me for you."

"And you think that's why I've let you stay? They may have bought you for that, but it doesn't mean I'm going along with it. You're staying because…" Nicky waved his hand around a bit, searching for something, some words he didn't have. "Because I can't send you back to the meat market. Doesn't mean I'm going to sink to the level of using you, though, it's not right. Forget it and go to sleep."

Michael considered him for a long moment. "Where do you want me to sleep?"

"What?"

"Where do you want me to sleep?"

"There isn't anywhere else but the bed. You're too big to fit any other place."

Again Michael licked at his lips. "And what do you want me to do?"

"Do? I don't know what you're going to do, but I'm going to sleep now. I have to be up really early in the morning." He got into bed, pulling the duvet up to his chin. He rolled onto his side, back to the center of the bed, same position he always started the night in. "Get in, if you're going to. Then I'll turn the light off."

It was a long moment before he heard Michael slipping into some boxers and a T-shirt then felt the bed dip behind him. When he reached round to pull the light cord that hung over the bed he saw Michael's black slave T-shirt hanging over the end of the bed and his own old Jimi Hendrix one stretched across his chest. "Night," he said, before settling down.

"Good night," came the quiet reply.

* * * *

Much, much later, Nicky turned over in bed to find his nose squashed against Michael's shoulder. Michael still lay on his back, arms folded over his chest. It was obvious that he was wide-awake and, more than likely, that he'd never been anything else. "Go to sleep," Nicky said. "Everyone feels better after they've slept."

"I can't." There was more emotion in those two words, hidden in the dark and the quiet, than Michael had shown since Nicky had first seen him.

"Why not?"

"Scared." And the sentiment was thick, palpable, in his voice, tearing at it till it was sure to rip apart.

"You're safe here."

"But what if…if I'm asleep and…"

"I'm a really, really light sleeper," Nicky said softly. "If anything happens, if anyone else comes around, I'll be awake in an instant, and I promise I'll wake you. But remember, no one can hurt you now, not unless I say so, and I'm not saying it."

He heard Michael inhale harshly before letting it go in a long, long breath. Ten minutes later, they were both asleep.

Chapter Two

Nicky placed the mug of coffee on the small bedside cupboard and crouched down next to where Michael still lay sleeping. He'd partially opened the curtains and now, in the early morning gray light coming through the gap, he could see Michael's face. The skin was drawn tight across his cheekbones and there were dark circles under his eyes. But he was sleeping at last and that had to be good.

Nicky really didn't want to wake him, but he thought it was infinitely better than Michael waking to a note on the table and an empty flat. He sighed, then called Michael's name once, and again, louder this time. He could see the exact moment Michael's brain reached consciousness, and the reality of his situation kicked in. Michael was instantly wake, his eyes wide and wary.

"It's okay, there's nothing to worry about," Nicky reassured him. "You're okay."

Inhaling hard, Michael looked at him as though he were a lifeline.

"It's okay," Nicky said yet again. "I only woke you to tell you that I have to go to work now. I didn't want you to wake up alone."

"But..." Briefly Michael's eyes went to the window. "It's dark, early."

"Yeah, I know, really early. I work odd hours. I'm going now, but I'll be back at about lunchtime. Stay in bed, sleep, you seem like you could use it. There's bread and cereal in the kitchen, help yourself to that and anything else you can find. Anything—food, drink, TV, another bath, more pain pills. Do whatever you want, use whatever you want. But..." He wiped across his mouth before going on. "You can't go out. You mustn't. I'm sure you know the consequences if someone sees you and I'm not there. No one would stop them, they'd...you know what they'd do to you. Stay in and stay quiet." Again he paused as Michael continued to stare at him. "The thing is, people know you're here, and they know I won't be. So don't answer the phone or the door, not to anyone, not for any reason. Keep quiet so it seems like the place is empty, and don't open up for anything. Miss F downstairs will head off any trouble if she can, will ring me if she can't. She knows you're here, and I'll explain it properly to her when I get back. But for now, this morning, just stay here. Stay safe. Okay?"

"Okay." Michael nodded.

"When I go I'm going to lock all the doors and windows," Nicky said. "I'm not locking you in. I'll leave a spare set of keys on the table, with my phone number. Call me if you need to. I'm locking everyone else out. You understand?"

"Yes." Michael nodded again. "And thank you."

"It's okay, you're welcome." Nicky got up, stretching out his protesting legs. "I'll stop by the supermarket on the way home, stock up. So eat anything you want, although there isn't much here, and Michael..." He smiled down at the man in bed. "You really are safe here. Go back to sleep and enjoy it."

* * * *

"Work right on the tips of your toes. Don't let the raised leg dip, Ingrid. Feel it reaching out to mark the line of your body, to amplify your extension."

Beam work. It had to be done most days, if not every day. The repetitive, formulaic work that the girls could almost do with their eyes shut. And that was the whole point of it, this boring routine that formed the bedrock of their skills on the beam. No big tricks, no acrobatics, but it built an innate knowledge of where the beam was, and where the girl was in relation to it. They literally could tell where the end of the beam was with their eyes shut, knew where it was when coming out of a pirouette.

If you could do that out of a pirouette, you could also do it out of a back somersault or, harder still, a front sommie. This kind of beam work built the confidence and grace that was the backbone of any routine. It was essential. The girls knew it, so did Nicky.

Nicky also found it as boring as they did, but you couldn't let standards slip. "Carrie, you're rushing it, you know you are."

"But I'm doing everything I'm supposed to." She huffed. She was arguing more with herself than Nicky. She knew exactly how important this was.

"It doesn't look right though, does it?" He shrugged.

She huffed again, scowled at him then went into an arabesque, right at the very end of the beam, one that was as beautiful as any he'd ever seen—stretched from the arch of her foot to the tips of her fingers.

"Now that's more like my girl." He grinned at her and she tossed her head in acceptance.

"Okay, everyone. Finish that repetition and then it's races to get your blood going before we get down to some real work. Same two teams, a forward and backward walkover on the way out, any dismount with a twist, and three pirouettes on the way back."

"Three!" There was a chorus of groans aimed at him. Pirouettes were damned hard to do at speed and these races were deadly competitive.

"Three. And you can't use your hands on the mount."

"Nicky!" they shouted.

"Losing team has to clear up at the end of the session. Oh, and two repetitions each. Go," he yelled, and they were off.

He walked over and sat on a pile of mats, watching them. If the slow beam work built confidence, these games took away any fear.

After a moment, Adeline came and sat next to him. He knew by the way that she'd absented herself from the races that she wanted to talk to him, but now she seemed nervous, and that wasn't like her. Not around him.

"What is it?" he asked, after a long moment.

She pulled at the sweatshirt in her hand, twisted the cuff into a spike, before deliberately putting it down and placing her palms on her thighs. "My mum told me what happened last night. What they did for you, what they...bought you." She trailed off, licking at her lips.

"About the slave?"

"Yes." She nodded. "Mum didn't think you liked it, that you weren't happy."

"It's not that I wasn't happy," Nicky started carefully. Adeline was sixteen — a remarkable sixteen but still only sixteen. "I appreciate the mums wanting to give me something to say thank you, but really the cakes you all made were enough. I didn't need anything else."

"And now you're angry?"

"No, of course not. It's just that, well, to be honest, I didn't want a slave. I have you all, and my work here, I don't want any distractions. I don't have time for them."

She licked her lips again and started to reach for the top but sat on her hands instead. "But a slave's meant for..."

"I know what a slave is meant for."

"And you don't want that?" She stared up at him, her eyes wide and round and trusting.

"No." He shook his head. "Really, I don't. If I want sex," he said the word carefully, flat and neutral as he could. "Then I want it with someone I care about, someone that means something to me."

"But..." She looked away, blushing hard but determined to go on. "With a slave you can...have everything you want."

He thought about what he wanted to say. This young woman was pushing herself to be honest with him and ask what she wanted to know — the least he could do was give her the same respect. "I don't think it should be about one person taking everything they want, it should be about two people sharing."

"About sharing and caring?" She stared at him again.

"Yeah, you said it perfectly. Sharing and caring."

"Oh, I am glad," she said with feeling. "I didn't want to think that you would...that you wanted... I am glad you want more."

"I'm no knight in shining armor." He smiled.

"But you're no dirty pervert either." She grinned back. "Are you very cross about the slave?"

"No, not cross. I was annoyed last night, but nothing's as bad in the morning."

"What are you going to do with him? The slave."

"Well." He scratched his head. "Right now I have absolutely no idea."

"You aren't going to..." She dropped her voice low, leaning into him. "...kill him or something?"

"Good God, no." He laughed out loud. "No, really, no."

"So what are you doing to do?"

"I don't know but I'll think of something," he rushed on to reassure her. "Till I do, I'll just carry on feeding him toast and eggs."

"Does he like toast and eggs?"

"I think he likes most things."

"You think he likes coconut cake? I could make him one."

"Sweetheart, I don't think you're meant to make slaves cakes."

"Oh," she said. "But..." Again her attention was on him. "You're not mad? Not at my mum? She was really worried all night."

"No, honestly. You tell your mum I'm not mad at anyone, especially her. Say I appreciate the gesture and I'll work something out. Okay?"

"Okay." She nodded.

"We going to do some work now?"

Again she nodded, already getting up.

"Right, you horrible bunch," he said to the whole gym. "Since you all cheated like mad, the whole lot of you lost, therefore you can all clear up." He clapped his hands together over their indignant protests and smiled. "Before that, the Twilight fans can stay here and work beam with Beth. Those with the brains to hate sparkly vampires come and work vault with me. We have champions to make."

* * * *

Nicky rubbed at the back of his neck, huffing. He was tired and his shoulders ached from supporting the girls in the new vault they'd been working on for the last few weeks. If they didn't get it right—if he didn't support them exactly where it was needed so they learned to do it for themselves—then there could be a very serious accident.

Trouble was, he couldn't complain about anything. If he was tired, Lord only knew how they felt.

The session was nearly over, which meant they could all take a break. He'd head for the supermarket—they had to go to school. He thought he had the better alternative, but he also had an unwanted slave to deal with. Suddenly school seemed so simple.

"All right, we're done for this morning," he said wearily. "Hit the showers now, but don't forget to work as hard at school as you did here. You did well, ladies."

He watched as they left, still running, and continued to be amazed at their energy.

Beth walked over and leaned on the wall next to him. She was a couple of years older than him, small, with short, dark hair and a wide, expressive smile. She had two cats at home, was always carrying a few extra pounds and had been hopelessly in love with their ballet teacher for years. Hopelessly because Max was very, very gay. It didn't seem to make any difference to Beth. She knew but couldn't change how she felt.

She glanced over to check all the girls had gone then got a can of lemonade from her bag. They had a deal that no one drank fizzy drinks, even if they were diet ones. "Ingrid isn't making any significant progress on the double forward walk-over on beam. She should be by now." She handed the can to Nicky.

"Did you try everything I suggested?"

"Yeah, and a few of my own but..." She hitched a shoulder, nothing else needed.

"She needs forward elements." Nicky sighed.

"I know. Will you try with her?" She held her hand out for the can, slipping down the wall to sit on the floor. "You have a way of getting them to do things I can't. Do them and believe in their own ability."

"Okay. We'll leave it for today and I'll try tomorrow."

"Or leave it for a couple of days—I know you have other things to think about." She looked up at him. "How is he?"

Nicky sighed again, big and over dramatic, and slid down next to her. "Scared shitless and frighteningly ready to let me fuck him. They sure ground in the idea that's all he's for."

"But it is, isn't it? That's why people have slaves— for sex," she said levelly.

"I know but..." He shook his head, teeth fixed into his bottom lip.

"So you're not going to have sex. Have you thought anymore about what you are going to do with him?"

"I don't know. I honestly have no fucking idea." Again, he took the can, almost snatching it out of her hand. "It's all so fucked up. I don't want him, I don't need the hassle, I want to just dump him but..."

"But what? You can if you want, or are you too bothered by Mrs. Bygroves?"

"Stupid cow of a woman. I don't know how her daughter can be so nice when she's so twisted and up her own arse. But it's Mrs. Milton we have to be really careful with. You know if she pulled some strings, we'd never work again—no matter how good our results are."

"So that's why you haven't kicked him out?" She watched Nicky, her focus fixed on his, and he knew there was no escape. They'd been friends far too long for that.

"No one should be that scared," he said softly.

"You can't stop the system. It happens, there's nothing people like you and I can do about it." She dipped her voice low. You could never be sure who was listening.

"But if you'd seen his face..."

"I can imagine," she said, then huffed. "No actually, I can't imagine. Just like you, I've stayed as far away from things I can't change as I possibly can. Like most people, I don't want to see the true cost. But I guess if you're faced with it up close, you have to see. Doesn't mean you want him staying, living in your home though, does it?"

"No, I really don't, it's way too small and..." He wiped across his eyes a little too hard.

"But you're not going to throw him on the street?" Beth let the question hang.

"How can I?" he said with feeling. "We all know what would happen to a slave out there."

"So?"

"So you and I are going to sit here till we think of something that will get him out of my flat, and stop him being my responsibility, but not put him in danger."

Beth finished the rest of the lemonade and rooted around in her bag for a bar of chocolate, broke it and gave half to Nicky. They ate in silence. "You know," she said at last. "I have a feeling we're going to be here for a really long time. We should order pizza."

"Shut up." Nicky threw the chocolate wrapper at her as he pulled himself up. "I have food to buy and things to do." He took a deep breath, scrunching up his face as he thought. "Will you come round tonight, after the evening session? I want you to meet him and…"

"And what? Why do you want me to meet him?"

"To tell me I'm not crazy for letting him stay?" He huffed again, a loud, exasperated sound. "I don't fucking know."

"I think that's your new favorite phrase." She got up, searching round for her sweatshirt.

"That's because I don't know anything anymore."

"Don't worry." Beth patted his arm, leaving her hand there for a moment. It felt warm and comforting. "I'll come back with you later, and it'll all work out in the end. I have no idea how, but I'm sure it will."

Nicky had no idea either, but he hoped she was right.

* * * *

Nicky wasn't sure what to expect when he got home, loaded down with bags of shopping. He unlocked the door and stuck his head round, looking for Michael.

There was no one in the tiny kitchen, so he dumped the bags on the table and went to find him. The living room was empty as well so he headed for the bedroom.

Michael was standing against the wall, as far from the door as he could get.

"Hi, how you doing?" Nicky started. "Have you eaten yet? I know there wasn't much here but I stopped at the supermarket on the way home and..." It was then he noticed the way Michael's chest was heaving. "Are you okay?"

Michael pressed his palms flat against the wall behind him, nostrils flaring. "I didn't know who it was," he said very quietly.

"Shit, sorry, man." Nicky cursed himself. He'd scared the crap out of Michael that morning, telling him not to let anyone in. Of course he was scared now. "Sorry," he repeated. "Next time I'll knock or call out or both. It's only me and...sorry. Are you okay?"

"Yes." Michael nodded, taking fast, small breaths.

"Hungry? 'Course you are. Come on, let's go eat." He led the way back to the kitchen, cursing himself under his breath as he went.

It was easier to sit at the small table, eating their way through a pile of sandwiches, than Nicky had expected. At first Michael ate fast, furtively pulling food toward himself. But after a while he glanced up at Nicky and slowed down, not attempting to hide what was on his plate anymore.

It was easy, without the awkwardness Nicky had anticipated.

"So what did you do this morning?" he asked. Suddenly Michael's shoulders tightened and again Nicky cursed himself as he tried to smooth the reaction away. "Did you have a bath? Did the boiler actually work two days in a row?"

Michael's faced softened, although he didn't actually smile. "Well, it was kind of lukewarm, but that was okay. It was good." He nodded.

"What else did you do?" Nicky pushed the bag of fruit over.

"I..." Again there was a hesitation. "I cleaned up, tidied everything away and then...sat here."

"Why didn't you watch TV?"

There was a long pause before Michael spoke again. "Because we were told not to touch anything without permission."

"I said this morning to watch," Nicky said gently.

"I didn't want to interfere in anything of yours. If I damaged something..."

"Hey, honestly, I have nothing worth damaging. Look at this place." Nicky opened his arms to embrace the tiny kitchen space. "I have nothing worth anything, you're welcome to whatever's here. Now, what would you like?"

"I'd like to go h..."

Nicky watched as Michael clamped down hard on himself, fear and pain flashing across his face, before he made it blank, his gaze dropping to his lap and his shoulders rounding.

And something hot and fierce fired in Nicky's belly. He hated that fucking reaction, that fleeting glimpse into how Michael truly felt.

He hated that fear.

"Don't you do that." He suddenly pushed himself forward, reaching across the table, angry with everyone that had made Michael that scared. "Not here, not with me."

Michael looked up, hesitant, his tongue pressed against his top teeth.

Nicky made himself think before he spoke. "You don't have to act like a slave around me. In here we're just regular people, and you can talk to me like normal. If you want to say something, if you want something, then you say. I might not be able to get it or do it but, for Christ's sake, say."

"But we're not two regular people, are we?" Michael said levelly, softly, his voice passive and compliant.

"Fuck it." Nicky heaved himself out the chair, turning his back to grip the counter top, dragging in air through his nose, as anger at the system flushed his face. He took a deep breath, and another, forcing himself to calm down before he turned back.

He stared at Michael and, for once, Michael managed to hold his gaze.

"You're right, we're not," he said at last, shrugging at the words. "And I don't like that situation one little bit. But right now I don't know what to do about it." He took another breath, holding it before he forced a smile on his face. "So I'm making a rule. In here we're just us, Michael and Nicky, no slaves, no owners. Okay?"

There was a long silence as Michael continued to watch him.

"Okay?" Nicky tried again, deliberately sitting down and modulating his voice.

"Okay." Michael nodded, just once.

"But? I can hear a 'but' in your voice, only you're not saying it, so I figure the rule isn't working. What's the but?"

"Okay, agreed. But…" Michael said, and this time Nicky could see him pushing himself to go on. "Why?"

"What? Why don't I want you as a slave?" Nicky didn't understand. Surely that was obvious?

"Why would you act like this?"

"That's easy. Because it isn't right." Again Nicky painted a smile on his face, but this time it was a little more real. "I'm no saint but I can't live that way, not with either of us acting like slave or master. I'd go crazy within a day and..." He huffed then sighed deeply. "Today I had a sixteen year old — who used to think I was Superman — look at me in a completely different way, because I took you home last night. I'm not Superman but I'm also not the dirty pervert she was starting to think I might be. No, I'm not doing what's expected of me. I'm not going down to other people's level. But I need you to help me out with this. I need you to be as normal as you can be and not act like a slave."

There was a long pause before Michael spoke. "It's hard not to when they..." He tipped his head to the side but didn't say anything else.

"Call me a coward, but right now I don't want to think about what they did or said to you. I just..." It was Nicky's turn to stop. "Can we just pretend we're regular people till I work out what to do? That way I won't go crazy, and life will be a lot better for us both."

"Okay," Michael said again. "But..." He pushed on once more. "Is that it? Is that all of your reasons?"

"I don't know." Nicky suddenly felt exhausted. He'd come home hungry and, yeah, a little anxious, but who wouldn't be with a stranger in their home? He hadn't expected or intended a big scene with buckets of emotions thrown all over the place. He did calm, and maybe boring, not this.

But he'd come this far, he might as well be honest. "I've been really scared and I don't like the feeling." He shrugged, not quite knowing what the gesture meant. "When I saw it on your face it reminded me, made me get angry. I don't like it, I don't want to see it, I can't deal with it." Again the shrug, this time with more of a question in the movement. "Can... I know you can't just forget all that's happened but can we try and leave the fear outside? Let's say that in this crappy little dump, you're safe and we're regular people?"

"All right." Michael nodded, and this time when his face softened it almost reached his eyes. He took a deep breath and pushed the words out. "If we're regular people, can I have the last sandwich, please?"

"Knock yourself out." Nicky smiled, knowing how much asking must have cost Michael. "I made three times what I normally eat. And help yourself to anything else you want. Try the TV."

Again Michael tipped his head, watching Nicky. "Well..."

"Say it or I might have to scream," Nicky said with humor lacing his voice. "If you're here, I want you to talk. I feel stupid otherwise."

"I'm not big on TV but could I borrow some of your books and tapes?"

Nicky snorted a laugh, deliberately relaxing back into his chair. "I don't think you'll be impressed with the tapes. There are a few films in amongst them, but most are hours and hours of women's gymnastics, going back years."

"That's what you do, right? Something with gymnastics." Michael reached for the sandwich and ate quickly.

"I'm a coach. I've built an elite squad of eight girls. They're really good. That was supposedly the reason their mums bought you for me, because we wiped the floor with everyone else at the Regional Championships."

"Is that why you left so early this morning?"

"Yes, I work odd hours. An early session before they go to school, another afterwards. They don't get much time for anything else but at this level, there's no choice. Not if they're serious about it, and they are, they really are. They're an amazing bunch."

"That's why you have all the tapes?"

"To get ideas, to see past stars, to watch techniques, to see what we're not doing right. That sort of thing."

"And the books?"

Nicky grinned. "That's just because I love owning them. There are all sorts, fiction and non-fiction."

Michael took a deep breath, hesitated then asked, "Can I read some?"

"'Course you can, you should have just taken them."

"I did think about it." Michael ducked his head a little. "But I didn't know if you had a system for where they're kept and they're obviously valuable, as they're so old."

"Valuable?" Nicky laughed. "They're old because I pick them up in junk shops or markets. None of them are worth anything. I just like books, all books. You'll find ones in there on pretty much anything you can think of."

"So I can just rummage through?"

"Sure. I keep meaning to put them in some kind of order, only I never quite get around to it. But I kind of like the thought that someone else other than me wants to read them."

"Thank you," Michael said softly. "I... Thank you. For everything."

"Just because a situation is shit doesn't mean you can't try and make the best of it," Nicky said seriously. "I'll do my best, I will. And I talked to Miss F downstairs before I came in, explained the situation. It turns out someone she knew was taken as a slave when she was a little girl and she got all protective of you. Get this? She's going to bang on the ceiling with a broom to warn you if someone comes around and she can't stop them coming up the stairs. I can't see many people getting past her, but it gives you a warning."

"What should I do if someone does come?"

Nicky sat and thought for a moment. "I don't think it'll happen but, if it does, there's not a lot you can do. No one has the right to come in, not if we've locked the doors. Just..." He thought some more. "Don't give them an excuse. Don't leave any windows open, don't have a pan boiling on the stove, nothing that anyone could say was a danger. If Miss F bangs, turn everything off, go in the bedroom and close the curtains. She'll have already called me, so I'll be on my way."

"You're going to lot of trouble for me," Michael said cautiously.

Again Nicky shrugged, a gesture, he realized, that had become as common as his response of 'I don't know'. "Like I said, I don't like the look of fear. But now you have Miss F on your side and, I promise, I'll try not to scare you anymore, okay?"

"Okay." Michael nodded.

"So, what sort of books do you like?" Nicky asked. "I'll try and pick up a few next time I see some."

* * * *

Nicky stopped Beth as they got to the top of the landing, getting her to take a step back. He knocked on the door loudly, knuckles banging, before opening it and calling out at the same time. "It's only me," he said, pitching his voice to reach as far as he could.

Beth stared at him, eyebrow raised.

"Only fair not to scare him anymore than I have to," Nicky said, as Michael appeared from the living room, book in hand.

"Hello," he started to say, before he fell silent when he saw Nicky wasn't alone.

"It's all right," Nicky reassured him. "This is Beth, my assistant coach. She's one of the good guys." Michael remained still. "Honestly," Nicky went on. "She's okay. If she can help, she will."

"Hi." Beth thrust her hand forward, seemed to think better of it and sort of waved at Michael instead, blushing brightly in embarrassment.

Nicky pointed at her face, grinning widely. "And that is why she's my best friend—because her blushing is way worse than my half-red face."

"Shut up." Beth slapped his arm, but the blush didn't fade. "I only put up with him because he's gay," she said to Michael. "Hello," she tried again. "I'm Beth."

"Michael." Michael tipped his head at her.

"Has everything been all right this afternoon?" Nicky asked.

"Yes, it's been quiet." Michael stood awkwardly by the door.

"Good. You want a beer?" he asked them both.

"Oh yes." Beth beamed, already heading for the fridge and collecting three bottles. She flipped them open skillfully and passed them over. "Have you got anything good to eat?" she said, but she had already gone straight to Nicky's cupboard and opened a family size bag of popcorn before he could say anything. She sat at the tiny table, took a handful and pushed the bag across the table toward Michael, nodding at him to sit.

Slowly, with a quick glance at Nicky, he moved forward to perch opposite her and took a few kernels for himself.

Beth looked at Nicky and waited till he sat in the last chair. "So?" she said, and again waited. Nicky didn't notice the pause as he stuffed his mouth with popcorn, but Michael seemed to.

This time Michael's gaze went slowly from one to the other and he moistened his lips. "I know you don't want me, a slave," he said carefully, words and tone measured. "So if you've changed your mind about keeping me safe and you brought a friend because you're going to tell me you're selling me, then I'd rather you did it quickly instead of building up to it."

"No, no. Fuck, no." Nicky waved a startled hand in Michael's direction, even though he still had his beer bottle in it. "I'm not taking you back to the market."

"So what are you going to do?" Michael asked, his fist clenched tight on the table.

"I guess…" Nicky sounded a little sheepish, even to himself. "I guess I brought backup to tell you I still have no idea what to do."

Again Michael's attention went from one to the other.

"Nicky and I talked this morning, and since then we've both been trying to work out some sort of solution that's good for everyone and…" She shrugged.

"I'm not going to sell you because I know what'll happen to you, and I can't be responsible for that." Nicky stared directly at Michael. "But I can't just tell you to leave or even give you some money and set you up somewhere else."

"You know how it works," Beth carried on. "Any slave is fair game to all the perverts in the world, unless their owner is there to stop them. Any time, any place that you're away from Nicky, you're vulnerable, and there's a hell of a lot of people who'll take advantage of that. You're seen as a legitimate target. I can't protect you, only Nicky can. If we got you a room on your own, it would soon be common knowledge and, without Nicky to stop them, they'd turn up and...you know what they'd do. You can't run because there's nowhere to run to, can't hide because there's nowhere to go."

"When we thought about it, Beth and I, decided that there must be some group out there that helps, like the French Resistance during the war." Nicky took up the explanation. "Trouble is, we've never even heard of the existence of one and, if it does exist, we have no idea how to find it. I'm no one special – I don't know anything outside a gym. Unless I look it up in the phone book I have no idea where to start."

"And if the authorities find out Nicky is looking then he's in a hell of a lot of trouble," Beth said.

"I can't protect you if I'm in prison," Nicky finished simply.

"So we're back to having no idea what to do." Beth shrugged and finished her beer. "We're not exactly the greatest rescuers, are we? We'd certainly get thrown out of the Superheroes gang."

"But there's one tiny good thing we have going for us," Nicky went on. "There's no rush. If you stay here, you're safe. That gives us time to…I don't know what. Maybe a lightning bolt will hit, and we'll suddenly think of an idea. Maybe something will change or we'll hear of a way to get you somewhere safe. We're not giving up, no way. But whatever it is, we have a bit of time. Till then, you just have to stay here and stay quiet and wait, I guess."

"It may not be the world's greatest plan but it's the best we have at the moment." Beth shrugged before managing to stretch across to the fridge for more beer without actually getting out of her chair.

"Sorry?" Nicky offered.

Michael's breath seemed to catch in his throat, and he spluttered, looking down for a long, long moment as he breathed hard. "Sorry?" he said, when he eventually lifted his gaze. "I really don't think you have to say sorry to me. By now I was expecting you to have… But you didn't, and you haven't. Instead you feed me, tell me to help myself to anything of yours, go out of your way to make me feel safe and talk to me like a regular guy. No, I really don't think you should say sorry to me."

Nicky realized that was the longest speech he'd ever heard Michael make. "Well," he said simply. "You are a regular guy, aren't you?"

"Yes," Michael breathed out the word, his voice wobbling. "Just a regular guy—although I was starting to forget that. Thank you for reminding me."

"No problem." Nicky smiled.

"Although." Beth pushed over more beer, even though the two men had hardly started on their first. "It would have been really amazing, and downright useful, if you weren't a regular guy. If you were in the Superheroes gang, it would solve all our problems.

I'm not sure what super power it would be best for you to have, but any would be better than nothing."

"Don't take any notice of her." Nicky threw a popcorn kernel at her head. "She always talks bollocks."

"I..." Once more Michael's voice started to tremble and splinter as he took gulp after gulp of air.

"Hey." Nicky gave him a smile of support. "Have you eaten yet?"

"No." Michael shook his head. "I didn't like to..."

"That's good because Beth's an amazing cook."

"Me?" She looked scandalized. "Why have I got to cook?"

"I'll help," Nicky assured her with a huge, fake smile.

"What have you got?" Beth asked. "Let me guess, it's pasta and salad yet again."

"What?" Nicky laughed. "It's cheap."

Beth started to argue back until they were interrupted by Michael's quiet question. "Can I help?"

"Of course you can," Nicky said. "Regular people lend a hand and help in a regular sort of way."

Chapter Three

Usually, after the first training session, Nicky would hang around at the gym doing the endless clearing up necessary—restacking mats and putting equipment away, talking to people, watching the younger girls work, trying to decide if there was anyone with enough potential to make it to the elite level or just deciding if there was anyone he could work with. If that didn't last long enough, there were always errands to run, things to do to fill the time. Somehow sitting at home, on his own, never filled him with enthusiasm. He did enough of that in the evenings.

Now...now things were different. Now he went home between sessions. At first it was just to check on Michael—who knew what could have happened while he was working? But he could admit he liked the way the fear in Michael's eyes faded when he got back.

He didn't like seeing fear on a gymnast's face, or that of a naughty child's or in a slave's eyes.

Fear had no place in anyone.

But Nicky was used to living alone, being alone, and the novelty of Michael always being there soon wore off. Not that Michael was difficult to live with. On the contrary, Michael always seemed really careful never to intrude on Nicky's quiet, never make a fuss or a mess. He hardly spoke unless spoken to, did his best to keep out of Nicky's way and generally was as considerate as he could be.

Which was nice, really nice. Until it wasn't.

"He creeps around in the shadows," Nicky moaned to Beth. They were sharing a bag of crisps in the gym, after the girls had gone. Michael had been living in Nicky's flat for just over a week. "He's like a mouse, creeping around the edges of the room making odd little scratching noises."

"He's a bloody big mouse," she scoffed.

"Fuck off." He reached into the bag again and took all the unbroken ones he could get. "You know what I mean. He's like Mr. Shadow-Man, Mr. Agree-With-Me-Man. It gets on my nerves. Why can't he just be...?"

"Be what?"

"Be normal."

"Because he's a slave, and he knows it," she said in exasperation, all but laughing at him, only to stop when he turned his scrunched up, unhappy face toward her. "Did you ever ask him how long he was at the Slave Preparation Center?"

"No," Nicky admitted. "I don't want to know."

"I don't either," she conceded. "Don't even want to think about it, but he was there, and you know they'd have trained him their way. So now he thinks he got lucky and has an owner that doesn't hurt him. He also knows that can change anytime you want—piss you off and you can hurt him. No wonder he does everything he can to stay out of your way and keep you sweet."

"But I don't like it," Nicky protested. "Creep, creep, whisper, whisper. It's not natural. I know he's there, but he's always just out of my line of sight, like an itch, a worry, crawling up my back. His presence…nags at me, like it's alive, crawling under my skin. I need my space, a chance to unwind. Somewhere I can slob out with no worries, no cares. He's invading my space, and it makes me itch."

"Hell, you must be a miserable bastard to live with." She snatched the bag back.

"I don't want to live with anyone," he said, indignantly.

"But you're stuck with him, so suck it up and make the best of things instead of whining like a toddler."

"I'm not whining."

"No, of course not." She grinned at him. "And that is nothing like a sulky face you have going."

"Fuck off." He grinned back.

"Is that your new phrase for the day?"

"It beats 'I don't know', my old favorite." He gave a huge sigh as he licked at his fingers. "What am I going to do? His…quietness is driving me crazy."

"Have you told him?"

"What am I supposed say?"

"Oh for God's sake, you idiot. How is he meant to know if you never say anything?"

"I…" Nicky didn't have an answer for that.

"Tell him not to whisper and creep around, tell him to act normally."

"It's not just that. He leaves whenever I enter the room—he sits on the bed and reads when I'm in the living room, scuttles out of the bathroom if I go near it, takes a step back whenever I pass."

"He wants to give you your space." She looked at his disbelieving face and sighed. "Come on, I bet you have your miserable 'leave me alone' expression on whenever he sees you. No wonder he stays out of your way."

Nicky hitched a shoulder, acknowledging what she said. "So what do I do?"

"Well, what do you want him to do? Stay out of your way or come in and talk to you?"

"I...I don't fucking know." He delved down in the bottom of the bag, balling it up and throwing it at their feet when he came up empty. "If he has to be there then he might as well be in the same room as me."

"You sure? You aren't going to freak at that as well?"

"No." He sighed, big and dramatic. "It has to be less creepy."

"So tell him, invite him in again." Beth suddenly stared at him suspiciously. "You did invite him in, didn't you?"

Nicky could feel the blush of embarrassment crawl up the unblemished side of his face.

"Sometimes you're so stupid you make me ashamed to know you," she said in a matter of fact tone. Then she pulled herself to her feet, brushing the crisp crumbs off her legs. "And do it nicely, be nice to him. The poor bastard deserves it."

Nicky watched her as she walked away and thought she was probably right. He should be nice.

* * * *

True to his word, he invited Michael in to watch an old film that night, chatted with him about the book Michael had just read, asked — very nicely — what he wanted for dinner. Did the same the next night and the next. Kept it up till the day he came home for lunch tired, irritable and with a thumping headache. Nothing had gone quite right that morning. The gymnast he'd been trying to teach a new combination of somersaults on bars had become heavier each time he supported her through the move, till she'd smacked him under the chin on the last attempt.

He'd sworn he could see double, but Beth had said he was being melodramatic again. Instead he'd slunk off home without clearing up, sulking.

When he got in he'd reached first for the bottle of whiskey, hidden from no one behind the bread bin, then the book on dinosaurs he was sure he'd left on top of the fridge. Neither were where they were supposed to be. "Michael," he yelled, louder than intended. "Have you seen my book and my booze? I need them."

Michael stopped in the kitchen doorway, filling the space. "I think I put them away?"

"You think?"

Michael looked self-conscious as he stepped from one foot to the other. "I'm sure I put them away."

"Away where?"

"The book's in the living room, and the bottle is on the shelf over there, where you keep all your other booze."

Nicky sighed, found the whiskey, then went to the draining board for a glass. It gleamed, clean, shiny and metallic but completely devoid of glasses. He sighed again.

"In the cupboard on the left," Michael said quietly.

"Why do you have to clean up all the time? A bit of dirt and disorder never hurt anyone," Nicky said, as he got a glass and knocked back his first shot.

"Sorry." Michael was no louder.

"I mean, look at this place, it's frigging unnatural. Don't you think?"

"Yes, unnatural."

"Two men living in a tiny space don't make it onto the cover of *Beautiful Homes* and where the fuck is my book?"

"I put it away in the living room."

"But here is where it's meant to be." Nicky slapped the top of the fridge, making it shudder alarmingly. "Things should be where they're meant to be, not just moved." He could feel his voice rising, the heat building in his cheeks, the whiskey rolling in his belly.

"Yes, they should stay where they are," Michael all but whispered.

Nicky knew another shot of whiskey was too much on an empty stomach as soon as he swallowed it. He searched around for some bread to soak it up. The bread bin was suspiciously clean, with no lurking moldy bits at the back. "Goddamn it, would you just fucking stop cleaning up."

"Sorry." He could scarcely hear Michael now.

"I mean, it's fucking..." Then Nicky turned and saw Michael's face. The fear was back. "Shit, sorry." He rubbed at his cheek. Beth had said be nice, and she was right. He was failing in every way. He searched in the back of a cupboard and found a reassuringly stale donut, which he ate in four quick mouthfuls. That was better. Now he had to make it right with Michael. "I'm sorry," he said again.

"You don't have to apologize to me," Michael interrupted. "I was trying to...be useful. Only I'm not as good at anticipating what you want as I thought I was. But if you say what you want done, I'll do my best."

"That's just what I don't want." Nicky flopped out in the kitchen chair, knees spread wide. "I don't want you trying, I don't want a housekeeper."

"I know. You want your space back. I'm sorry."

"No, that's not it." Nicky huffed again and thought about what he did mean. Beth had said be nice and also to talk to Michael. It was good advice. "When I was younger I saw a few films set in American colleges, where they had roommates. I thought we'd be like that—sharing a beer, talking crap, watching stupid TV. Not you cleaning up after me."

"Sorry."

"Why do you do it?" He looked up at Michael, not angry, just wanting to know. "Is it just to keep me sweet?"

"Well…" Michael shrugged. "It's something to do, and keeping you happy can't be a bad thing."

"I know it must be boring as shit, alone here all day, but clean and tidy don't make me happy."

"I get that now." Michael nodded. "I'll stop."

"No, don't do that." Nicky gave a tired smile. "Cleaner is good. Just…we do half each and not so much. Cleaner but natural. What do you say?"

"Whatever you want."

Nicky let his head fall back and groaned noisily for a long time.

"What?" Michael ventured.

"Stop it, just stop it. Stop being nice to me and stop agreeing with me all the time, it's driving me nuts." He sat back up, staring at Michael. "I actually like having someone to talk to, but not if you agree with everything I say. If you hate a book I suggest, say so and say why. Same goes for films. We don't always have to watch what I like, or eat what I want to eat or… Stop saying yes and be honest. Be yourself."

There was a long pause. "Are you sure that's what you want?" And Nicky knew that was a huge question for Michael to ask.

"Hell yes," Nicky said emphatically. "Stop creeping around in the shadows, start making a noise and be yourself. If we're going to be roommates, you have to have opinions on things. If you love something say so, same for anything you hate."

"Well," Michael said, just the hint of something at the corner of his lips. "I hate tomato soup."

"Really?" Nicky sat up straighter. "So do I, but Beth said normal people love it and you'd find it comforting."

"Comforting?" And now Michael seemed bemused.

"Her word, not mine. How about chicken soup?"

"Not bad if you add enough pepper. Even better if you make your own."

"You can make chicken soup?"

"I don't know but you're bound to have a recipe book," Michael said. "And—" He hesitated a moment again. "If I piss you off again, you'll say?"

"Only if you do the same."

"I'm not sure I can…"

"Tell me the most annoying thing about living with me, right now, right this second, or I'll buy a case of tomato soup and make you eat the lot," Nicky demanded in his most pretend-serious voice. The one the girls laughed at.

"Wet towels on the bed," Michael said quickly.

"Huh?" Nicky hadn't been expecting that. "Really?"

"And always on the side I sleep."

"Okay. I promise to leave them on my side?"

"Or hang them on the bedroom doorknob if you can't make it back to the bathroom."

'If you can't make it back to the bathroom'. Was that a hint of a proper criticism? If it was, it was the first Michael had ever made. That was more like roommates.

And just like that, Nicky thought, things were better.

* * * *

Not always. There was no soaring music or silly pranks, and there were a ton of hiccups along the way. But after that day the atmosphere seemed to change without Nicky realizing what had happened. It was like a toothache — you only noticed it when it was there, didn't always remember it once it had gone. The feel inside his tiny flat changed — the mood between them became easier and so much more comfortable.

Comfortable. That was a good word. They were comfortable together and Nicky sort of forgot that it had ever been any other way.

He found that he liked sitting together, Michael's big body fighting to fit in the chair at the tiny table, as they shared bread and cheese for lunch, talking round in circles about a book that Michael had just read. Michael was easy to talk to, easy to be near.

Even the complete and utter weirdness of sleeping with a stranger in his bed hadn't lasted long. The first few nights he'd lain awake for long stretches, looking up in the darkness at the ceiling, trying not to think as he listened to Michael breathe. But surprisingly quickly, he'd found himself waking just before his alarm clock went off, same as he always had, having slept full and soundly.

For a while he worried about that as well. Shouldn't it have been more difficult? Had he been so desperate for company that he'd take anyone, even a slave, forced to be there? But that would have been about masters and slaves and this was about...

Nicky didn't know. All he was sure of was that he felt comfortable with Michael. It was weird but he was too dumb — or too sensible — to question it. They were comfortable together. He'd go with that.

After their first week together he'd said to Michael, as he brought coffee just before he left, that he wouldn't wake him anymore so he could sleep on. That had felt like the right thing to do, there was no need for them to both wake up so early.

But Michael had shaken his head, even as his hand went out for the mug. He seemed to like knowing when Nicky was gone, liked knowing when he was alone. No, he obviously didn't want to wake up uncertain. Now, sometimes Michael would get up while Nicky was in the shower and make coffee for both of them.

It had been easier than Nicky had thought possible to fall into such a simple routine. To get used to the company away from the gym. Not that there had been much time away from there. He'd pretty much had to work all through the last few weekends as two of the youngest girls were taking part in a junior demonstration. There was no need to worry, no real pressure, but Nicky — and the girls — had wanted to be as ready as possible.

This weekend he'd earned his rest and he was going to enjoy it.

* * * *

He yawned, deep and wide, not bothering to cover his mouth, as he started the inevitable clearing up after the last Friday session. Stack the mats, sort out the water bottles, find more hand chalk then, maybe, he could go home. Beth had long since deserted him, going to the cinema with an old school friend instead.

It was just as he was going for his second mega yawn that Adeline sidled up to him. Sidled — there really was no other word for it when you added together the small steps, the furtive looks over her shoulder, the nervous twitch and the blush on her cheek. "What have you done?" Nicky smiled down at her.

"Nothing. Nothing I shouldn't have." Her blush grew. "Just, here." She thrust a plastic box at him.

"Okay." He raised an eyebrow as he took it and tried to lift the lid.

"It's coconut cake. I mean, I made coconut cake."

"Thank you," he said, wondering. "You know I always like cake."

"It's not for yo—" Her face went white. "Yes, of course it's for you. I made you coconut cake. But you can't eat it here or give Beth any. You have to take it home. It's for you to eat at home. And..." She licked at her lips. "I made a lot. One person might not be able to eat it all."

"Oh." Nicky suddenly caught on, pressing the lid firmly back in place. "I shall take my eat-at-home cake home and eat some. And if there's any left, I'm sure I'll find someone who wants it."

"Does he...does anyone else who might eat it like coconut cake?"

"Sweetheart." Nicky kissed the top of her head as he squeezed her shoulder. "Anyone would like your cakes. You make the best ones I know."

This time she giggled and ducked her head, obviously delighted. "I just...just enjoy the cake," she said, glanced up at him. "Is he, I mean, everything is okay, isn't it?"

"Yes," he reassured her gently. "He's just fine."

"Good." She smiled, and the next moment she was already running out of the gym.

Nicky put the box on top of his jacket and went to finish up. The world wasn't such a bad place when there were people like Adeline in it. And she really did make fantastic cakes. It was such a shame that she loved to bake but couldn't eat them. But then, he figured, her loss was his and Michael's gain.

* * * *

"Hey," Nicky called out as he let himself in. "Sorry I didn't warn you I was going to be late, but the gym was a tip tonight. It also stinks. Who knew young girl's sweat could be so...stinky?"

"It's okay." Michael looked over. "I started dinner. I hope that's okay, I figured you'd be hungry."

"That's not okay, that's brilliant. What are we having?" Nicky dumped his things in the corner and tried really hard not to yawn any more.

"Well," Michael's voice dropped, hesitance creeping into it. "There wasn't much left so I've just, sort of, cooked up what I could find."

"Shit, why didn't you say?" Nicky asked. "I should have gone shopping but I never think of it and...what have we got?"

"Baked potatoes with a very small bit of cheese and frozen sweetcorn?"

"Wow, that sounds interesting. But..." He produced the plastic box with a flourish. "We have cake. Adeline—the most amazingly graceful gymnast I've ever seen—has decided to make you cake. She's passing it off as for me but it's yours by rights. Want to share?" He grinned at Michael as he passed it over.

"Yeah," Michael said softly, his gaze on Nicky. "I'll share. But I don't get it—why did she make me cake?"

"Well, I suspect she's not only worried about you but also a bit fascinated." Nicky started to pick at the edge of the cake, eating with his fingers and sighing in pleasure. "Think yourself damned lucky. Not only does she make amazing cakes but they used to be exclusively for me."

"Worried about me?" Michael shrugged. "That idea takes some getting used to." He forced out a reproduction of a light hearted grin that looked more like a grimace. "But now we have a meal fit for kings. Potatoes, a hint of cheese, sweetcorn and cake," he said as he started to serve up.

"And I promise I'll go shopping tomorrow." Nicky put the box on the table and collected cutlery and beers, before sitting down. "What did you do today?"

Michael passed a plate over and joined him at the table. "I finished *Moby Dick*. I haven't read that since I was a kid. Then I went searching for something different." He tipped his head, gazing at Nicky, and there was an almost-smile just touching the corners of his lips. "I'm now reading about the beginning of sheep farming in Australia. Man, you have some weird books."

"But interesting. You have to admit they're interesting." Nicky smiled back, much more whole-heartedly.

"Have you ever been to Australia?"

"Yeah, right." Nicky laughed. "You know no one gets out of this country, the borders are locked down tight."

"So...a deep and sincere interest in sheep?" Maybe there was even a hint of humor in Michael's tone now?

"Not so you'd notice."

"Then, for God's sake, why?" And there it was—the first genuine smile Nicky had ever seen on Michael's face. It might only have been small and brief but it was real.

"Because it had a pretty cover? Because it smelled nice? Because it was cheap? I don't know, I just like owning books. You wait till you find the ones about snakes. I hate the creepy-arsed creatures, but I have at least a couple of books about them." Nicky liked the look of that smile on Michael's face—it sure beat the fear.

"I don't think snakes have an ass."

"Oh come on, everything has to have an arse. Where else does the poop come out? If they didn't have an arse then it'd all collect up inside till they exploded or something." Yes, Nicky liked the smile way better than the fear.

"They're not going to explode," Michael started.

And that's how it had become between them—easy and, more surprisingly, comfortable. They could talk about important things but they also did comfortable so much better than Nicky had ever imagined possible.

* * * *

Next morning there was a reversal of their normal roles. It was Michael waking Nicky with a mug of coffee, looking worried. "Hey," he said softly, which didn't make sense, as the intention was obviously to rouse him. "I don't know if your alarm didn't go off or you just overslept or whatever, but it's late. Well, late for you. You're usually half way out the door by now."

"Thanks," Nicky said, sitting up and taking the mug in both hands. "But I don't have to be in until later today. It's Saturday, thank God. We only have one training session on a Saturday, so it usually starts later and then a whole day off tomorrow."

"Oh shit, sorry." Michael started to back away, looking as if he'd been caught doing something bad.

"It's okay. We were working the last few weekends but it's back to normal now." He sipped at the hot liquid, enjoying the idea of it more than the actual taste.

"You should go back to sleep." Michael hovered, reaching out to take the coffee back but seeming to think better of it. "I should get out of your way."

"It doesn't matter. I have things to do." Nicky stretched and scratched at his side before getting out of bed. "First thing is going to be breakfast and then a hot shower that I actually don't have to rush, for once. After, I reckon that..." He stopped, looking at Michael. "Do we have anything left for breakfast?"

"Yeah, there's some bread and stuff, don't worry," Michael reassured, leading the way out to the kitchen.

"I really need to get organized or domesticated or both, don't I?"

"Well." Michael hesitated, the tip of his tongue caught between his teeth. But it didn't last long. "How about I do some of that? Seeing as you're at work a lot of the time."

"You already do," Nicky said softly. "You think I didn't notice?"

"It's not like I've got much else to do all day." Michael shrugged. "But..." Again that slight hesitation. The one that Nicky wanted gone, wanted Michael to feel comfortable enough to let go. "How about I do something with the washing?"

"Shit, you're brave if you're prepared to tackle the stinking, living mess that's the dirty clothes bin." Nicky laughed as he started to make toast.

"I tried to do it a couple of day ago but..." And this time Michael was half smiling when he paused. "Your washing machine got the better of me. I couldn't figure out how to make it work."

"That's because Mavis is an old, loyal but fickle woman. She only works for me and even then, only if she feels like it."

"You call your washing machine Mavis? Man, you're..."

"Go on." Nicky handed over a plate of toast. "You'd say it to a regular roommate, so say it to me."

Michael stood stock-still and stared at Nicky for a long, long moment. "You're..." He took a deep breath, held it then exhaled fast and hard, as though making himself take the step. "You're weird." He smiled, and this one nearly made it all the way to his eyes. "But I like your weirdness."

"Good." Nicky grinned. "I like my weirdness as well, and, for that, I'll introduce you to Mavis."

* * * *

Michael was standing, hands on hips, glaring at the washing machine and muttering things under his breath when Nicky got back after training.

"Hi, how was your morning?" he asked, then saw Michael's face. "Not good." He shook his head.

"Mavis hates my guts," Michael stated.

"I wouldn't go that far." Nicky put his things on the table before walking over and crouching down in front of the machine. "She did start for you."

"And she washed, rinsed and spun."

"Really?" He glanced up at Michael. "Wow."

"Yes. But now she won't open and I'm actually calling the thing 'she' and a name." Michael shook his head and glared some more.

"See, that's your problem. You upset her." Nicky ran a gentle hand across Mavis' top. "Did the tall man call you names, baby?" Nicky all but cooed. "It's all right, he didn't mean it. I still love you." He patted her twice, tried the door and it opened instantly. He gave Michael a blazing grin as he stood up. "You just have to be nice to her. She can't help being old and noisy."

"I..." Michael just carried on shaking his head, his gaze going from Nicky to Mavis. "I have no words, not for either of you." He grabbed the basket and emptied the wet clothes into it, then stopped and stared at Nicky again. "Where should I put all this? There's no room in the bathroom."

"I usually put it on the clothes airer in the little space outside the front door, at the stop of the stairs," Nicky said, as he started to unpack his bag. "It's a real suntrap, things dry quickly there and the place doesn't end up full of wet washing and smelling of damp." He suddenly became aware that things had gone every still and quiet behind him. "Michael?"

Michael was standing with the basket in his arms, chewing at his lip, his focus fixed so hard on the front door that he could have burnt holes through it.

"What's the matter?"

Michael's chest heaved, the rise and fall of it emphasized by his thin T-shirt.

Nicky tried again. "What is it?"

"I haven't been outside, not since, since…"

"Not since you first got here," Nicky said softly. "You must be going stir crazy stuck inside all that time."

Michael stood stock still, his gaze fixed on the door. "I looked out the window, saw the sun, thought about how it would feel on my face. Fresh air, the wind on my skin, the taste of the dew in the morning but…" He turned, staring again at Nicky, wide-eyed. "I'm safe in here. Safe as I can be," he corrected himself. "I'm not safe out there. But to feel the sun…"

"So why don't we go outside together and hang up the washing?" When Michael didn't move, Nicky dragged the airer out from beside the fridge, opened the door and took a step out. "Coming?" he asked softly, then turned his back to give Michael the chance to follow without being watched. "No one ever comes around here apart from us and Miss F, so we're unlikely to see anything except the back of the laundry." He kept up a running commentary, talking about nothing, as he heard Michael come out. "People used to park here before the bowling alley closed, now it's just my car, the potholes and the odd stray animal."

He started hanging things over the bars of the airer and, after a pause, Michael joined in. The gym clothes Nicky wore all the time, Michael's T-shirt that screamed slavery, his jeans, their socks and underwear mixed together. The sun warmed the small space as the task kept them busy and Nicky's inane chatter filled the air.

When they were finished, Michael turned his face up to the sun and closed his eyes. It was the happiest Nicky had ever seen him.

"You know how crap I am at most domestic things?" Nicky didn't want to break the mood but just maybe he could make things better for Michael.

"Not so crap." Michael opened his eyes. "You got Mavis to give up the washing and you actually own an airer and know what to do with it."

"Okay." Nicky grinned. "You know how amazing I am at domestic things? Well, I managed to remember that there's no food left and brought sandwiches home with me. Now that is amazing." He went to get the food from his bag but still witnessed the exact moment Michael tensed. "It's okay," he reassured. "There's no one here and I only have to reach in to get them." For the first time ever, Nicky was grateful that his home was so small. "Here." He handed a parcel to Michael before sitting on the top step to unwrap his own. It oozed with ham, cheese and salad. Wonderful.

Michael came and sat next to him, a perfect position to catch the sun. Nicky ate slowly, giving Michael time to savor being outside. When he got up to make coffee he waved Michael back to the step but made sure he stayed visible through the open doorway. And there were those words again, words Nicky was just getting used to—good, easy and comfortable. Words that were worth having in his life.

"So what did you do this morning, apart from upsetting Mavis?" Nicky asked.

"I decided to sort through all the books, see what's stuck at the bottom of a pile or behind a cupboard. But I didn't get far. You have a hell of a lot of books."

"Did you look under the bed? There're a lot of boxes there. Oh and Miss F has some in her place."

"How do you know what you have?" Michael asked, bewildered.

"I sort of remember what I bought, can't, hand on heart, say where they are though."

"You need a system, some organization. I spent ages looking but I couldn't find the book on classic motorbikes you told me about."

"It's in..." Nicky scrunched up his face, thinking. "Last I saw it was in the bathroom but that was months ago. I have no idea now."

"I'm telling you, it needs a system. Same goes for the videos. I tried one labeled 'Travels in The Outback' only to get the women's gymnastics world championships from 1985."

"Did you watch it? That was a really good year," Nicky said enthusiastically. "It was Elena Shushunova and Oksana Omelianchick right down to the wire. Both from Russia, they were neck and neck and eventually tied which is downright ama—"

"Nicky," Michael interrupted him forcefully.

And Nicky stopped, mid flow, because that was the first time Michael had ever been even slightly firm with him. He grinned—that was definitely better. "What?"

"I'm saying you need a system."

"You'd rather watch Travels in The Outback than Oksana?" Nicky's smile grew.

"I'm saying you probably couldn't find Oksana and you need a system." Michael hesitated, but not for long. "You want me to create one?"

"Would you?" Nicky grinned wildly. "Hell, yes. If you find the tape with the floor final from that year, I'll worship you forever."

"You really love your job, don't you?" Michael said, reaching for his coffee.

"Yeah, well. Everyone thinks I'm crazy working with girls, seeing as I'm gay. But it's not about that, should never be about that. I love gymnastics. Helping them improve, seeing them gain confidence and grow. I think they're the most amazing bunch of people — of any age or sex — I've ever met. What's not to love?"

"Don't knock it," Michael said. "Getting paid for doing something you like has to be something most people wish for."

Nicky stopped eating, turning to consider Michael and the scene around him. He was leaning back against the step, his neck stretched as though to get as much sun on as much skin as possible. The wet washing behind him, the smell of detergent from the laundry next door wafting through the air, the sound of angry car horns a distant distraction. Nicky knew nothing about Michael, nothing except he was a slave and he was starting to lose the fear in his eyes.

"Did you have a job, before?" Nicky asked.

"Me?" Michael twisted his head round toward him. "Yes, I had a job and a life, once upon a time."

"Tell me." Nicky didn't demand an answer, his question was gentle, genuinely interested. "And tell me about your accent. You're sure not from around here but I can't place it."

"No, I'm not from around here." Michael sat up straighter, his shoulders rounding. "I'm from an ordinary town in America."

"You're American?" Nicky knew he was staring, knew he looked stupid with his eyes bulging and his mouth frozen in a ridiculous O shape.

"Yeah." Michael rubbed at his face, sighing.

"Wow, I just...wow. I..." Nicky made himself stop and breathe. "I've never met anyone from another country, except at gym competitions. But...American? Wow. How the fuck did you end up here? Like this?" He waved a hand toward Michael's slave T-shirt.

Michael stared at him. "Please, I'd really like to know."

Again Michael sighed, picking up the wrapping from his food and crushing it into a ball. "I grew up in a non-descript town, studied hard, became an accountant, just like everyone expected me to—the good boy. Got a decent job in New York with a big firm, I was settled for life. But I was so bored." He passed the ball of paper from hand to hand, twisting it in his fingers. "Unlike you, I hated my job and I longed for adventure. I dreamed about going to sea, dropping out and becoming a hippy, even joining the circus. Only trouble was there was no one thing I wanted to do passionately. I just didn't want to be stuck in an office for the rest of my life."

When the silence went on too long, Nicky prodded. "But from that to here?"

Michael shrugged, still playing with the paper. "It sounds like madness now, a horror story, but it started off normal enough." He sat back, knees spread wide.

Nicky thought he looked ready to talk at last.

"I decided to find out what I wanted to do before I fossilized. So I took a year's sabbatical from my job and went backpacking. I didn't plan a route or book places to stay, I just went. My family freaked, said I'd gone crazy, but I was only taking a year off. Anyway, I bummed around a lot of places, had some fun but no real adventures and I wanted an adventure." His voice sounded slight, almost wistful, until he shook himself. "I'd always been fascinated by this country. I guess anywhere you're not allowed to go is fascinating, and the borders here are so tightly sealed—it's so secretive. So I came to see what it was like at the border, see if it looked...I don't know, how I thought it would be. Different from everywhere else, I suppose."

Again he paused, tipping his face up to the freedom of the sky before dragging his attention back down. "It all seemed so exotic, so mysterious. I'd heard stories about the place but most of them turned out to be wrong. You don't have dragons or wizards, just slaves and ordinary citizens who aren't allowed out, let alone to say what they think."

"Is that what the outside world thinks of us? That we have magic?" Nicky asked.

"I don't suppose the politicians do, but stupid things get whispered around. It was magic or aliens mostly."

"Either is better than what's really here," Nicky said. "Just fear and more fear."

"Yes, just fear," Michael agreed.

"Tell me the rest, if you want to."

"Not a lot left to say." Michael shrugged. "I wanted to see, I went out on my own, got too close to the border even though I'd been told not to. I got lost in the thick woods, and the soldiers who picked me up said I'd crossed over into this country. I don't know, maybe I had, but there was a fucking high wall, and next second I'm on the wrong side of it, tied up, thrown into the back of a truck and being driven further in."

"They patrol the outside of the wall, even though they aren't supposed to," Nicky said, thinking it through. "The army says it's to make sure the wall's intact, and that no one can get in or out. They must have taken you when they were out there."

"Makes no difference," Michael said. "I'm still in here with no rights and no way of getting help."

"I'm sorry, I'm really so very sorry," Nicky said, and it he meant it. "What's happened to you is just appalling."

"Not your fault."

"It feels like it," Nicky admitted. "Feels like I should apologize for my whole country."

"No, just those in power."

"And those that agree with them."

"Yeah, those too," Michael said. "Thing is, I can't even tell anyone back home that I'm still alive."

"The government here won't admit you exist. If they did they'd have to explain how you got here and send you back."

"That's what I assumed." Michael collected up the litter, stacking it in a pile. "Instead they took me to the Slave Preparation Center then sold me, making an unexpected profit for themselves."

"Your adventure couldn't have turned out much worse, could it?"

Michael actually laughed at that. "Yeah, Nicky. It really, really could have been worse. A whole fucking heap worse. If I hadn't ended up here with you. If it wasn't for you..."

Nicky couldn't help ducking his head as he felt his face start to flush at that.

"Now both halves of your face match," Michael said softly, reaching out to touch Nicky's cheek gently.

Nicky blushed all the harder. He thought it was the first time Michael had touched him. He knew he hadn't touched Michael — he hadn't wanted to see any more fear in his face.

"It's a birthmark, right?" Michael's fingertips ghosted across the side of Nicky's face, down from his eye to his chin, before he lifted his hand away.

"That's right. I've always had it, just like it is now." The birthmark was on the right side of Nicky's face. Not nasty or ugly looking, no raised or angry spots. This was a soft, muted, almost subtle wash of color. It really did look as though he were blushing but just on the one side. It was only when you saw him face on and saw that it never faded, that you realized it was actually something more.

"It..." Michael angled his head to the side, really studying Nicky. "It suits you, suits your personality."

"Half a red face? I don't know about that, but I think it helped form my personality," Nicky said, honestly.

"You got ribbed about it when you were young, at school?"

"Not ribbed." Nicky sucked in a deep breath. "They made my life a living hell because of it. I can tell you a million half-faced blushing jokes."

"It must have been tough," Michael said, his voice strangely calm, as though he were truly trying to think how it would feel.

"Add that to being gay and..." Nicky shrugged, the implication obvious.

"They knew? You came out at school?"

"I didn't choose to come out, but..." This time Nicky frowned as he thought about it. "It was rather I got thrown out of the proverbial closet and the door locked behind me. Everyone knew."

"And made it tough for you?"

"Not the best time of my life, that's for sure."

"I'm sorry, sorry you had to put up with that."

"I don't think you should feel sorry for me," Nicky said, with a raised eyebrow. "Not under the circumstances."

"Okay." Michael nodded in agreement. "But only if you don't feel sorry for me. Like I said, it could be a whole hell of a lot worse."

Nicky thought that was a pretty remarkable way of looking at things. Most people would have wallowed in self-pity — he was sure he would have. But Michael was different. Michael was trying to find the best in things, the simple pleasures. If that was the sun on his face, Nicky would try and give it to him.

"Well," Michael said decisively. "I like your birthmark. Like I said, it suits you."

"How can having half a pink face suit someone?" Nicky asked, crinkling his face up in confusion.

"You're..." Michael smiled, soft but full. "You're weird but in a really nice way. The mark goes with that."

"I have a weird but nice birthmark?"

"Yes, you do. It suits you."

And Nicky couldn't argue, not when Michael smiled like that. "Okay, if you say so." He pulled himself to his feet, picking up the sandwich wrappers. Michael went to collect the coffee mugs but Nicky stopped him. "No, I'll do it. You sit in the sun for a while longer."

Michael looked around him, suddenly not so sure. "What if someone comes?"

"Miss F will give us warning and I'll be just inside the door, washing up." Nicky went in, putting the mugs in the sink and running the water while he continued to talk. "You can guard the washing, make sure the Oompa Loompas from the laundry don't steal it."

"See what I mean?" Michael leaned back across the steps again, tipping his face up and stretching out his legs. "Thieving Oompa Loompas and an interest in sheep. Weird, but in a nice way." The smile just touching the edges of his mouth seemed almost natural there.

"And incredibly domesticated." Nicky wiped his hands on a tea towel. "Not only do I know how to use a clothes airer, but now I'm going to go shopping and buy food. Lots of food. And beer, we need lots of beer."

"Oh, okay," Michael said, the smile fading away as he sat up. "Do I just leave everything out here while you're gone?" He gazed through the door, back inside the small confines of Nicky's home, and it seemed to Nicky as if a spark of light had been put out inside him.

"Yeah, unless, do you want to come with me?" Nicky asked.

"Am I allowed to?"

"You can do whatever I say, as long as you're wearing the slave T-shirt." Nicky was decisive. "But you have to remember to stay right close to me. As long as I can see you, I can protect you."

He watched as Michael weighed up the possibilities—a trip out of the few tiny rooms he'd been trapped in for days and weeks versus the fear of being outside and less safe. "It's only the supermarket, nothing special," he said, coming out, tea towel still in his hand.

"Eighteen." Michael glanced up at him.

"What?"

"I can take eighteen steps from your front door to the back wall of the bedroom. Eighteen. It would be…good to take a few more," Michael said gravely.

Eighteen. Nicky didn't know that, had never been bored enough to find out. "Then let's go shopping," he said, just as seriously before giving a big grin. "You can stop me buying too much junk food, especially any kind of savory snack. I have a real weakness for those, but the girls say it isn't fair if I get to eat them and they don't."

"Or you could just eat them here?" The smile was back on Michael's face, small, and you had to look for it, but it was there.

"I knew there was a reason I liked you," Nicky said, grabbing his wallet before he locked the door after him.

* * * *

"I'm sorry. I'm really, really sorry," Nicky said, in the car on the way home. He gripped the wheel so tightly his knuckles had turned white, and he knew, downright knew that as his face blanched, his birthmark stood out more vividly than ever. "Fuck, I'm so very sorry." Nicky glanced across at Michael, taking more time than was safe, but he had to see his expression. Had to see how he was reacting.

"Watch out," Michael ordered, fists curled on his thighs, staring straight ahead.

Nicky looked back at the road and managed to swerve just in time so he didn't hit the car coming right at him. The car, whose lane Nicky had invaded. He sucked in a breath, holding it close as he thanked whatever powers had saved them. For long moments he concentrated on the road but then he had to say it again. Had to. "I'm sorry."

"Not your fault," Michael said at last, pushing the words over his teeth with a real effort.

"I should have got there faster, should have been more attentive. I should have—"

"Nicky," Michael said, as decisive as Nicky had ever heard him, authority and the knowledge he was right seeming to infuse every syllable. "It was me that screwed up. We both know it."

"No, I should have…"

"You told me to stay with you. It was me that went looking for chocolate cereals. It was my mistake."

"But I said go look for them and —"

Michael turned in his seat, face set in the same blank mask he'd worn when Nicky had first met him. Only now Nicky could see the effort it was taking to keep it in place. "I got overconfident, no, stupid. I was stupid and I let myself forget."

"And I let you," Nicky said softly, almost to himself.

The shopping trip had started off so well, so normally. It had been just like every other time Nicky had gone to that supermarket, except this time he had someone to share the visit with. Someone to talk to.

"Is there a reason you have four packets of toilet paper and two huge bags of pasta?" Michael had asked quietly, so no one could hear except Nicky, as he poked about in the trolley.

"The toilet paper is buy one get one free and the pasta is almost half price," Nicky answered, surveying the shelves. "Plus pasta is cheap, nutritious and filling. What's not to love?"

"And the olives?" Michael continued to push the trolley along the aisle. "I didn't think you liked olives."

"Seventy-five percent off. I adore a bargain."

"So I noticed." Michael had ducked his head, but not before Nicky had seen the smile, soft but real.

They carried on in that way, discussing the merits of different beers, how to pick the best fruit, what vegetables to get. Yes, there had been more than a few odd looks thrown their way, but that was more because Nicky was talking so comfortably with Michael, rather than the fact he was a slave. Slaves weren't that uncommon—although most tended to be kept under lock and key. You could see them on many busy streets. But they were very much kept in their place, very much the slave.

Nicky knew as many of the looks were mocking him for not knowing how to treat a slave 'right' as they were admiring of Michael. Admiring his possession. He'd pushed the thought to the back of his mind and went back to sorting through the packets of cheese till he found one that appeared perfect.

"I wonder which cereals are on offer this week," he'd asked, head still half in the chiller cabinet. "I hope it's the chocolate ones that turn the milk brown. I like those."

"I'll find out," Michael said, and Nicky hadn't thought anything of it. Not until he turned round, cheese in hand, and Michael wasn't there. For a moment he'd looked up and down the aisle, just absently wondering where he was. Then it had hit him.

Michael wasn't there. Michael wasn't within his line of sight, and if he couldn't see Michael, he couldn't protect him. Couldn't stop all those hungry eyes turned his way. Eyes whose owners had been stopped by Nicky's presence. But Nicky wasn't there now.

He'd pushed the trolley out of the way, ignoring the noise as it crashed into the shelves of soup, and ran up to the top of the aisle. Which way? Back was fresh produce, forward was dry goods. Cereals were dry goods, weren't they? He ran, heart thumping in his chest, and rounded the arm of the next aisle to see

Michael pressed up against a stand, surrounded by three eager looking men.

One was smearing a hand across Michael's mouth, pulling his lips obscenely out of shape, as his other hand reached out to grab at Michael's crotch.

Michael stood stock still, staring at nothing, letting it happen, but Nicky could see his chest heaving.

"Touch him again and you deal with me," Nicky said, amazed at how darkly calm, how intimidating his voice sounded. "I'm not given to sharing what I own."

"Yours?" One man said, as they all turned to face him. "You can't value your property much if you leave it out for anyone to use."

Nicky heard the words but also saw the hand fall away from Michael. "I made a mistake and misplaced my property, just for a moment. Do you really want to call me on it?"

"You should be more careful," the second man said. "There are a lot of people who'd like to play with him, your property."

"I will." Nicky let his genuine thanks seep into his voice. "Thanks for reminding me. I won't make that mistake again."

The men walked away then, a swagger in their step at what they'd nearly had, and magnanimity in letting it go.

Nicky had grabbed Michael by the arm and started walking him to the nearest exit. But Michael had caught their trolley as they passed, pushing it toward the tills, his attention fixed on Nicky, although he said nothing.

Nicky had never gone through check out so fast, never got it all in the car as quickly. Never driven away with an actual squeal of tires before.

"And I let you," Nicky said softly, almost to himself. "I let you forget the danger out there. I should have warned you."

"You did. More than once," Michael said, as they pulled up by the steps that led to the flat.

When Nicky glanced across the car the fear was bright in Michael's eyes. "Let's get inside. Leave the stuff and..." Then he was out, almost running round to pull Michael from the car. Next second they were both sprinting up the stairs. They didn't stop till they were inside with the door firmly shut behind them. But Nicky needed one more gesture, even if it was only symbolic. He shot both locks and slid home the bolt.

"Shall I put a chair under the handle?" he asked, half seriously.

"I think that's probably going too far," Michael said, but he stood as far away from the door as possible in the tiny kitchen with his back against the wall.

Nicky squeezed his eyes shut for a moment, then rubbed at them hard with the back of his hand. "I'm sorry. I just... I'm really sorry."

"No, it wasn't your fault. It was mine." Michael's voice was insistent. "I knew what could happen, what would happen. I was told often enough."

"But I should have stopped it. I should have —"

"No," Michael interrupted, firmer still. "The only thing you did was let me believe it didn't have to be like that." He dropped his head, his hair covering his face, and Nicky could hear him breathing hard. Eventually he looked up, his gaze soft on Nicky. "In here I feel safe, I can breathe and that's all down to you. In here I really feel like your roommate, not your slave and I truly thank you for it."

"It's the least I can do."

"But you didn't have to." Michael carried on watching him. "In fact you've gone out on a limb by doing it. I know the government wouldn't approve."

"I don't care what they think. I try to do what's right."

"Not many people would follow you on that one," Michael said simply. "You're doing what's right at a cost to yourself. That's…appreciated. But I got careless, I started to believe the way you treated me was the norm."

"I should have…"

"No," Michael interrupted again, gentler this time. "You reminded me what to expect before we went out. I heard you, but I didn't listen, not properly. The only thing you could have done to prevent what happened would be to treat me like they did. That way I wouldn't have forgotten."

"Is that what you want me to do?" Nicky asked, going on before there was time for an answer. "You want me to treat you like shit just to remind you? I'm not going to. I'm not going down to that level, not for you or anyone. I won't behave like that, not even if you want me to."

"I don't and…" Michael suddenly ducked his head again. When he lifted it this time, he was trying to smile. "I don't want you to change. I'm thankful for the way you are, but…" Again he attempted a smile that was soft and honest. "I like the fact you won't change, not even if I wanted you to."

"You're welcome, I think." Nicky scrunched his face up, trying to work what Michael had said. Right and wrong was easy compared to that.

"Just…" Michael sighed, a sigh from the heart. "Just remind me next time. Remind me what it's really like out there and make me listen."

"Now that I can do." Nicky smiled back.

Maybe things would be okay after all.

Only they weren't, not that day or the next. Michael would stare out of the window at the sunshine, but wouldn't go outside to hang up the washing that Mavis deigned to complete, not even when Nicky carried out the basket and started work. He wouldn't sit on the top step to eat lunch and had even arranged it so that Nicky brought the shopping up while he put it away.

On Monday morning, when Nicky got up for work, Michael climbed out of bed as well, making the coffee while Nicky showered. When Nicky left, Michael had looked strained and tense. After he shut the front door behind him, Nicky heard Michael close every lock, throw the bolt and, was that the scraping sound of a chair being dragged across?

It almost certainly was.

That night, as they lay side by side in bed talking, as had become their habit, Nicky thought it was time to press things. That was after the obligatory game of 'fight for the duvet' and Nicky's gentle reassurance that yes, he had locked all the doors, and no, Michael didn't need to get up and check. Then there was the shuffle, slip, slide trick Nicky played to get away from the heat Michael put out. But not too far away, the heat was kind of comforting. "What did you do today?" he began gently.

"I started organizing your books but I can't decide how to do it," Michael said.

"What are the choices?"

"Well, the obvious one is alphabetically, by author name. But as neither of us knows who wrote most of them, there didn't seem much point in that, as we'd never find what we want. So then I thought I'd do it alphabetically but within groups—science fiction, classics, westerns and separate ones for the non-fiction books." Michael counted off the categories on his fingers, and Nicky could see him just fine with the light from the street lamp coming through the thin curtain. "I'm going to have a special one for any books about sheep."

Nicky snorted softly at that. "I've seen you with the sheep farming book. You love the embossed cover just as much as I do."

"I don't know about that, but I'm beginning to get what you mean about the smell of old books. There's something special about it."

"It's magical," Nicky said, decisively. It was easier to say things like that in the semi-darkness—you didn't feel like such a fool.

"Yeah," Michael agreed. "The books can take you to any time, any place. The smell reminds you of all those possibilities."

"We need some more." Nicky pulled his hand out from under the cover and patted Michael on the chest. "Tomorrow, after the first training session, I'll take you to my very favorite junk shop and we'll buy books about times and places neither of us have ever known."

"No. No, you go. I'll stay here," Michael said quickly. "You don't need me with you."

"But you need to go," Nicky's voice was soft, coaxing. "You need to get out of here, just for a little while."

"No, I don't."

"Yes, you do, and the longer you leave it, the harder it'll be. We'll take the car, go straight to the shop, there's hardly ever more than one or two people there, then come straight back."

"But…"

"I'll stay right by your side the whole time. I'll remind you before we go what it's like out there and…" He paused, waiting for Michael to look at him. "I'll make sure you listen to me. Okay?"

Michael's eyes seemed like black holes in the dimness, dark spheres that dragged everything toward them.

"Okay?" Nicky pressed again.

"Okay." Michael's voice was a whisper but it was there and it had an edge of determination to it.

"I really will make sure you hear me and I'll be right there."

Michael nodded and this time his, 'okay', was stronger.

* * * *

They came back the following day with armloads of books, and pretty much all of them were Michael's choices. He'd protested but Nicky had waved it away, saying he loved all books, it didn't matter what they were about. Michael had been forced to accept the truth of that and they'd bought them all. He had even added an extra tattered one to the pile.

Nicky had started to protest about its poor condition then he saw it was a collection of sheep jokes. That had to be included.

"I can't believe they were all so cheap," Michael said, as he stacked them on the kitchen table. "Back home, in a second hand book store, they'd have been at least ten times the price."

"That's the joy of a junk shop as opposed to a bookshop," Nicky grinned. "Nothing in there is worth anything, except to the fool that buys it. Don't you agree?" But it was quiet behind him, making Nicky turn round. "Michael?"

"I was just thinking."

"Back home?"

"Yeah, something like that." Michael sighed.

"Doesn't seem so boring now, does it?"

"No." Michael gave a huff of abortive laughter. "Not as many books though."

And there it was again, Michael making the best of things. Nicky could have hugged him for it. "And today was okay?"

"Yes." This time Michael nodded. "Okay."

But that weekend he wouldn't go to the supermarket with Nicky and when he did, the following weekend, he was practically Nicky's shadow.

Nicky didn't mind—he kept one hand on Michael's sleeve the whole time they were out.

Chapter Four

Nicky knew he was being rude, that hiding in the kitchen with Beth while Michael watched TV in the living room wasn't polite, especially not when Michael had spent all day on his own. But Nicky needed Beth's help, and the kitchen was the only place they could get any privacy to go through all his papers.

Only they'd been there for hours already and there still didn't seem to be any way out.

Nicky sighed, then sighed again, rubbing at his face. "What if…?"

"What?" Beth asked. "I can't think of any more options. Move the money anyway you like and it won't make any difference."

"But," Nicky started but then couldn't think of anywhere to take that sentence.

"But nothing." It was Beth's turn to sigh. "You're in shit street, and I can't see any way out."

It was then that Michael knocked on the door. "I'm sorry to interrupt but I couldn't help overhearing some of what you said."

"I guess that's the joy of having doors that never quite shut," Beth murmured to no one in particular.

Michael glanced at her before his attention went back to Nicky. "It's just that I did use to be an accountant. Maybe I can help."

"Thanks, but I don't think so, not this time," Nicky said.

"Nicky." Beth hissed at him.

"No, it's okay." Michael started backing out. "If you don't want me involved I understand."

"Nicky." This time Beth barked out his name, an order in her tone. "For fuck's sake, you told me you think of him as a roommate. Well, stop treating him as a child and tell him the truth."

Nicky glanced from one to the other, looking lost, but saying nothing.

"Treat him with respect and tell him." Beth went on. "You can't hide it anymore."

Now Nicky's attention went to Michael.

"What can't you hide?" Michael asked softly, taking a step further into the room.

But still Nicky didn't say anything, as his fingers absently shredded an envelope.

"Fuck this." Beth shook her head at Nicky before turning to Michael. "He's broke. Completely and utterly broke and we can't figure a way out."

"Oh," Michael said, dropping into a chair opposite Nicky. "Have things always been this bad or has something happened?"

"Nicky?" Beth stared at him, one eyebrow raised. "You want me to do all the talking or are you going to man up and explain things to him?"

Nicky let his shoulders round and his head slump forward till he could bang it gently on the table top a couple of times. When he looked up it was with yet another sigh. "You. You're what happened."

"Me? What did I do?"

"Way to go, putting it nicely." Beth shook her head again but Nicky ignored her.

"I was just about managing for money before and then you came along and…" Nicky shrugged. "There were registration fees, other legal stuff and, well, you kind of eat a lot, and…" He shrugged again, more hopeless, more pathetic. "The money just ran out."

"Why didn't you tell me?" Michael implored.

"There was no point. It wasn't your fault and I didn't want you any more scared than you already were. I thought I'd figure something out." Nicky snorted, knowing he sounded full of self-deprecation. "That plan is working out as well as the one where we find a way to get you out of this."

"You should have told me," Michael insisted. "I could have…"

"What? What could you do?"

"Eaten less?" Michael shook his head. "Is that why you only buy things on offer?"

"No, that's habit," Nicky admitted. "I've never had much money."

"But now you have none," Beth said softly. "And you can't carry on. I'm sorry, Nicky, I can't lend you any more. I've given you all my savings. I don't have much left."

"No. No," Nicky insisted. "I can't take your money, not any more. I'll…think of something."

"It's really that bad?" Michael said, his eyebrows drawn together. "I don't know how the banking system works here but could we find a better investment, some way of getting around things temporarily?"

"I don't have any money left," Nicky said flatly.

Michael inhaled sharply, holding it in his lungs for the longest time as he stared at Nicky. Then he let it go, tipping his head in acceptance. "Then I guess you have no choice but to sell me."

"What?" Nicky stared at him as though he had two heads.

"There's nothing else you can do. I don't like it but I can see you have no choice. Thank you for trying for so long," Michael said formally.

"Oh fuck off," Nicky blasted, both dismissively, incredulous. "I'm not going to fucking sell you. What kind of bastard do you think I am?"

"One that has no choice?"

"Choice? There's always a fucking choice."

"Not if you don't have any money," Michael said softly.

"So I'll sell stuff, the books or something."

"You only paid peanuts for the books." Michael glanced around him. "And you have nothing else worth selling."

"Gee, thanks for reminding me. Why the hell are you so insistent about this?"

Michael rubbed his hands together then laid them flat on the table. "Because I'm being realistic. I'm the cause of the problem, you've done the best you could, for as long as you could, and I'm really grateful for that. Now you're at the end of the line, and we all have to accept the fact."

"So I just sell you? How the hell do I live with knowing what'll happen to you?"

"By knowing that you did your best and that there was nothing else you could do."

Nicky pushed up from the chair, his face white with anger. He turned, needing to get away, to stamp or shout or let it out somehow. Only there was nowhere to go in the tiny kitchen. After going full circle, he faced Michael and forced himself to calm down. "You've lived with me here, in this shoebox, for weeks now and yet you really think I could do that?"

Michael went to answer, stopped before the first word was formed, the first sound made. He tried again but once more stumbled. Then he looked up at Nicky with desperation in his eyes. "I pray you can't, but...I've prayed before and the prayers haven't been answered."

"I'm not selling you," Nicky said simply. "I couldn't live with that on my conscience. We have to find another way." Then he plonked back down in the chair, all his fight evaporating along with his anger.

"Thank you," Michael whispered, each word wobbling on its own axis.

"You're welcome. Now think of something."

"I—" Michael shook his head. "I have no idea." He glanced between them both. "How did the women that bought me, the mums, think that you could afford me? They must have known I cost a lot to keep, or didn't they know your financial circumstances?"

"Oh, they knew all right," Nicky said with feeling.

"So how did they think you'd manage?"

A glance passed between Nicky and Beth, one full of meaning. When the silence went on too long she asked, "Are you telling him or shall I?"

He sighed, sagging down into himself. "I was supposed to lend you out, no," he corrected himself. "I'm meant to rent you out." He caught Michael's gaze and held it. "I rent you out to them, the mums."

"Rent me out? For...?" It was Michael's turn to look between them. "For sex? Of course for sex. It's the reason anyone has a slave."

"For sex," Beth echoed. "They knew exactly what they were doing when they bought you. Nicky would get—what they thought of as—the hassle of housing and dealing with you every day. They'd have the fun of you when their husbands were safely at work. But Nicky would get a nice little income from you, especially if he rented you out a lot. To them it was a perfect state of affairs."

"And this is what you want to do now?" Michael asked, gaze going between them, chest heaving despite the fact the words were delivered with a thin veneer of civility and calmness.

"Would it be so bad?" Beth asked. "Free no-strings sex? We'd make sure they wouldn't hurt you and some of the mums are really attractive." She dipped her head for a moment, drawing in a breath, before looking back up. "Face it. The only way you get to have any sex is with Nicky's say so. If we did it discreetly, you could probably pick which ones and..." Again she dropped her gaze but had the decency to force her attention back to Michael. "It would solve a lot of problems."

Michael pressed his lips so hard together that the color bled from them and the muscles in his face shook with the effort. "I guess I can," he started to say, his Adam's apple working furiously.

"No," Nicky interrupted, shaking his head angrily. "No, no, no. You're not doing it." He couldn't stand the thought of Michael having to do that. Of Michael being with any of those women. The vehemence of his reaction surprised him. It felt hot and fierce. He wouldn't let that happen. Couldn't let it. Not to Michael. Not to his Michael.

"But I don't see what else you can do." Beth tried to add a voice of reason. "Things are so desperate now that..."

Nicky wheeled round to face her. "Forced sex is still forced sex, even if you aren't being hurt."

"But?"

He stared hard at Michael again. "Do you want to have sex with any of those women? Answer truthfully, not what you think anyone wants to hear or what's the right thing to do. Tell me the truth, do you?"

"No," Michael said, his expression little calmer. "But I will, if it means I get to stay here with you and not be sold."

"I'm not selling you, and I'm not whoring you out," Nicky said with finality.

Michael seemed to droop down, his hair covering his face, his breathing noisy in the quiet room. At last he looked back up at Nicky. "Thank you. Thank you for everything."

"I couldn't do it, it wouldn't be right." The simplicity of the statement sat right and easy with Nicky. "And stop saying thank you, it's boring. I get it, so enough now."

Without saying anything, Beth went to her bag and took out a half full bottle of whiskey. She put it on the table and found three glasses, filling them each part way and pushing one toward each person. It gave everyone in the room a chance to collect themselves and regain their composure. "So," she said, after draining her glass. "We've decided no whoring, and I agree, although I think it needed to be considered. But that leaves us back where we started—no money and very little food. Anyone got an idea?"

Both Michael and Nicky reached for their glasses, drinking quickly, as the silence went on.

"Maybe if I..." Nicky started and stopped, filling the glasses again. This time they all drank in unison. "I could try and work some more hours?"

"You already do all the girls are allowed," Beth sighed. "You could take on other classes, the less able, but when would you teach them? The only hours you don't work are when the kids are at school or in bed."

"Adult fitness classes?"

"Nicky, you're a gymnastics coach. You aren't qualified and don't know how to teach adult keep fit."

Nicky huffed in acknowledgment. "Okay, so I'll do something else. I must be able to get work elsewhere, in a shop maybe."

"In the few hours between first and second practice?"

"All right, in a bar. I don't work then. And stop being so negative."

"I'm negative, agreed." Beth unscrewed the lid of the bottle then seemed to think better of it and closed it again. "But when are you going to sleep?"

"What the fuck else am I going to do?" Nicky nearly shouted, and they both stared at each other.

"Can I do anything?" Michael broke the silence. "I mean, am I allowed to work? Other than sex."

"Well, technically you are," Nicky said. "You can do anything I say."

"So, could I get a job?"

"Yes, but it's not as easy as that."

"When is it ever in this country?" Michael snorted. "Why not?" He looked at Nicky who just stared back.

Again it was Beth that took over, explaining unpalatable truths. "You know what it's like for you out there. If Nicky isn't around to protect you by claiming ownership then you're fair game for all the perverts. It would be just the same if you were working. The boss would regard you as a perk he could use any time he wanted."

"Oh." Michael was quiet but he didn't give up. "Is there anything I could do from here, like working from home? I spend a lot of time doing nothing."

Nicky and Beth frowned at each other. "I don't know," he admitted.

"I suppose it's a possibility we could find out about," she said.

"It's that or I work somewhere with Nicky, somewhere he can watch my back. Is there anything I could do at the gym when Nicky's working? I can't coach but is there anything I could do?"

This time the frowns Nicky and Beth gave each other were confused, frustrated and laced with annoyance. "Why the fuck didn't we think of that?" Nicky demanded. "We're meant to be intelligent and we know the situation at the gym."

"Because we're fucking stupid." Beth grinned, reached across the small table, grabbed Michael's face, pulled it forward and kissed him on the forehead.

"What?" Michael asked.

"Our waterman died about seven months ago," Beth explained. "He fell off his roof, of all things, but he's never been replaced. He's called a waterman because he collects, washes, fills all the water bottles but he also does loads more. He makes sure there's hand chalk and anything else we need, acts as a handyman, getting stuff out and clearing up at the end of a session, things like putting the mats away."

"We've been trying to do it all since he died," Nicky went on. "But there's no time, and things are getting in a mess. The waterman also checks all the equipment. We've been doing that as well but when you're in a rush... I get scared we'll miss something and there'll be an accident."

"Why haven't they replaced him?" Michael asked.

"Because..." Beth's face lit up. "Mr. Pattinson, who's the owner's son and runs the gym, is a cheapskate and won't pay the going rate."

"This is good because?" Michael looked between their smiling faces.

"Because you don't have to pay a slave the going rate," Nicky explained. "In fact, you only have to pay them a fraction of the proper wage."

"But is it enough? Enough to feed me and the other things I cost?"

"If you work all the hours I do, we won't be rolling in money but it'll be enough." Nicky grinned, widely and happily for the first time in a long time. "Do you know anything about maintenance?"

"Not really." Michael smiled back, seemingly caught up in the mood. "But I'm strong, I learn fast and I bet you have more than one book about it."

"Oh I do, I have lots and lots of books." Nicky poured them all another healthy measure of whiskey.

"You think he'll give me the job?"

"One look at you and he'll be getting you to paint the ceilings in the changing rooms." Beth laughed.

That sobered Nicky. "But, Michael, you're going to have to be really careful. I'll be working, my focus will be on the girls completely. It has to be, for their safety. I can't have half an eye out for you."

"You won't need to, will you?" Michael asked.

"Pattinson isn't like his mother, the owner. He's out for what he can get, like all the rest." Nicky rubbed a hand over his face, thinking as he went on. "You can't go out of my sight and it has to be your responsibility to make sure you don't. I'll be concentrating on the girls. If he tells you to go get something, you say no. I won't let you, not without me. You don't even go to the bathroom without me coming along."

"Is it going to be that bad?" Michael asked.

"I hope not but...you know from the supermarket that it only takes a second for things to go wrong. You have to make sure I can keep you safe. To do that, you always have to be where you can see me, where I can see you and you can call out if you need me. I'll tell everyone my rules for you but people will try to get around them. You have to make sure they don't."

"I thought it would be different there," Michael admitted. "Seeing as everyone knows you. I thought that they'd respect that I was your property."

Once more it was Beth that took over. "Nicky is a very, very good coach — better than anyone else. Gymnastics is extremely competitive, even among the coaches. It can make for some intense feelings, especially jealousy, and if they can get one over on Nicky they might try it." She shrugged. "Apart from that, you're an attractive man. There are enough people who'd try something for that reason alone."

"Is this a good idea?" Michael looked to them both for an answer. "Should we go back to trying to find work I can do from here? The last thing I want to do is make things difficult for Nicky."

"No," Nicky said, suddenly decisive. "This is a perfect solution. Pattinson gets cheap labor, which will make his day, there'll be enough money for us all to eat all the time, you'll actually get out of this place on a regular basis but stay safe and..." He grinned at Michael. "I get to indoctrinate you with my love of gymnastics."

"You've already done that," Michael said. "I must have watched all your videos a dozen times."

"Good. But" — Nicky was serious again — "I think we...no, I, have to go in the right way."

"What do you mean?"

Nicky took a deep breath and reached for the whiskey bottle, pouring out a small measure for himself and the others. He scrunched up his face, huffed and shrugged at Beth as he held up the glass before clinking it with hers and drinking. "I'm going to have to be a muppet, aren't I?"

Beth suddenly turned bright red before spraying her mouthful across the table then coughing and laughing till she turned even redder. Nicky thumped her back unhelpfully as she wiped at her eyes. "Oh you're going to look such an idiot," she managed to say at last. "Everyone is going to have a ball laughing themselves stupid at you."

"But it will explain things," Nicky said. "Even keep the mums who haven't had the benefit of Michael off my back."

"You're right, it will." Again she started laughing, this time without the coughing and spluttering. "But you're going to be the butt of so many jokes."

"Wait," Michael interjected. "What's going on?"

"Nicky's going to be a muppet," Beth said brightly.

"Kermit the Frog or Miss Piggy?" Michael asked.

"It's a term of derision," Nicky explained. "A name you call someone who falls in love with their slave or thinks they have. It's a real put down, but it'll mean that they know there's no chance of me sharing you around. They'll laugh at me but back off from you."

"But that's...that's..."

"Another line of protection." Nicky shrugged.

"But you can't have everyone looking at you, thinking of you like that."

"It'll help keep their hands off you," Nicky said flatly.

"It's for the best," Beth agreed. "It really will help protect you."

"Just..." Nicky shrugged again. "Ignore me when I act like an idiot?" Michael stared at him, obviously not understanding. "I'm going to have to touch you, stroke you, hold your hand, gaze longingly at you. I don't know—whatever shit people do when they're infatuated with someone. I'm going to have to make it seem real and whisper sweet nothings in your ear." Nicky couldn't quite meet Michael's eyes for a moment because he wasn't sure how he felt about that. He wasn't sure how he felt about Michael.

That was one subject he really didn't want to think about.

"And then you can listen while all the adults laugh not so quietly and call you a muppet," Beth said.

"I can take that but I'm being Kermit." Nicky suddenly grinned, wide and easy. "Anyone calls me Miss Piggy and they're in deep shit."

* * * *

The music was so loud that it rattled the main doors in to the gym. The floor seemed to pulse with the beat and the walls vibrate.

"What on earth?" Michael said, but the question was in his eyes, in the shape of his mouth, his whole body.

Nicky grinned. Yeah, he had his own style of coaching. "Beth got here first. She's started the warm up."

"That's warm up music?" Michael's eyes got rounder.

"Rock—fast, loud and makes the girls want to move but it's precise, controlled. A brilliant warm up for a cold morning." He pushed the door open and led the way in.

The noise was even louder inside, bouncing across the space and thumping back into itself. The girls were all on the floor area, concentrating hard as they worked through a series of choreographed moves. It was almost like a dance but with simple gymnastic elements added. It was carefully designed to warm up every muscle and tendon while also focusing the mind. They moved completely in time with the music and each other, everything else forgotten, although several sang along with the track.

Michael and Nicky stood and watched as the song ramped up, taking the girls' movements with it. But even though everything was fast and frantic, it was also exact, accurate to within millimeters. When the music stopped the girls held their poses for a long moment then collapsed into a chattering bunch, all giggling and talking at the same time. They suddenly seemed much younger—true teenagers, rather than the poised young women of moments before.

"Ladies." Nicky switched off the CD player as the next track started, and everyone's attention turned to him. "This is Michael, my... He's the new waterman. He's big and strong and will fix things. Call him by his name if you need him, but he's not here to wait on you. So I'll say it again—pick up your own stuff, you lazy lumps."

All eyes were fixed firmly on Michael. Nicky could feel their interest like a living thing. "Girls." He added a pleading tone to his voice. "Do me a favor and leave him alone. You know I'll get in trouble if things aren't done right."

The girls might only have been teenagers but they knew the rules, knew how things worked with slaves. They carried on watching Michael, but did it a little more surreptitiously now.

"Right." Nicky rubbed his hands together. "Time to do some work?"

* * * *

A couple of hours later Nicky was working with Martha on a complex asymmetric bars dismount when he felt, rather than saw, Michael come to stand behind him. He talked Martha through the move, explaining how she could adjust her bodyline to make it even better, then stepped back. Together they watched her go through it again, concentration and control running from the tips of her fingers to the soles of her feet.

When she landed Nicky nodded and smiled. But she still had to ask. "Good?"

"Flawless."

"But not as graceful as Adeline." She pulled a face.

"Like I've said a million times before," Nicky's voice was soft, intimate. "You might not be as graceful, just like she's not as technically brilliant as you are. But with you both working hard to emulate each other, you're only getting better and better. You're both going to be unstoppable and I'm damned glad I'm not a competition judge."

"That will do." She grinned at him.

"Giant circles on the single bar?" It wasn't really a question, more an instruction. "You always need to work on your shoulder muscles."

"Yes, boss." She smiled again, then went to chalk up her hand guards before Nicky lifted her onto the high bar.

Again he stood and watched. "She's really good, isn't she?" Michael asked quietly. "They're all really good, way better than I expected."

"They're a fantastic bunch, not afraid of hard work or criticism. They work as a team even though, ultimately, they'll be competing against each other. Plus they nearly always stay positive. No one gets down for long."

"That's your doing. You set the atmosphere here and..." Nicky could hear Michael's breathing and he glanced back over his shoulder. "You're a really good coach."

"I know." Nicky' gave a cheesy grin.

"But..."

"What?" Nicky asked, suddenly concerned. "Have you had any trouble?"

"No, not in here," Michael reassured. "And that's the point. When we were in the office you saw the looks I got, but in here, with your girls...you set the tone, you treat me decently so they have automatically. Carrie said something about her mum and me, but then she just stopped and has been nothing but respectful. I didn't expect that."

"Carrie's mum was the one who bought you. That woman is a sly bitch. But Carrie is a good kid, a lovely kid." Nicky checked Michael again. "But apart from that, everything's okay?"

"Yes, I've finished everything you asked, and I'm starting to see what needs doing without bothering you. You're right—you really are focused on what's important, the girls."

"I have to be. But is this working out okay? Are you okay with the job?"

"Yes." Michael nodded. "I can do this. More than that, I think I'm going to actually like it."

"But remember to stay close to me." They'd both seen the way the manager, Pattinson, had looked at Michael. Both knew what it meant. Pattinson wasn't around often, especially not in the actual gym, but when he was in the building, Nicky made sure Michael never left his sight. When Pattinson was in the training room, he practically kept Michael in his pocket, and Michael seemed more than happy to be there. Nicky didn't question why he was more than happy as well. Wanting Michael close was a subject that came into his mind in the dark hours of the night but he wouldn't let himself think about it.

"Oh don't worry," Michael said with feeling. "I'm not letting you anywhere I can't see you."

Later that day when Pattinson passed through with his mother, the owner, Nicky pulled Michael close, his palm spread out between Michael's shoulder blades. Mrs. Pattinson smiled indulgently his way and Nicky turned his head, kissing Michael's neck.

It tasted salty, like a man. It tasted good.

* * * *

Michael pressed a hand to his back and tried to stifle a groan as he got into bed on Thursday night.

"What's the matter?" Nicky asked absently, putting on his bed T-shirt.

"I got flabby and out of shape sitting around here for all those weeks. Muscles ache that I don't remember having." Michael stretched out and tried to ease things. "Humping those huge mats around is hard going."

"Right, that's it." Nicky climbed in next to him. "You're training tomorrow with the rest of us."

"Training?"

"Mondays and Fridays, end of the second session, it's ballet training. The girls made Beth and I join in. You're on as well."

"Ballet? Me?" Michael all but spluttered. "Have you seen the size and shape of me? I'm hardly cut out for ballet."

"That's what I thought," Nicky said, pulling the duvet over. "But the girls made me, and it's the fucking hardest workout I've ever done. It half killed me the first time I tried it. Max, the dancer that teaches it, takes no prisoners. You'll be made to suffer, but don't worry, no one will notice. We're all too busy watching Beth moon over him."

"Why?" Michael rubbed at his aching back, trying to find a comfortable position.

"She's madly in love with him. Blushes whenever he looks at her. But he's gayer than I am. She has no chance. None at all."

"You're cruel to her. But I still don't see why I should suffer." Michael eventually settled on his back, arms on top of the covers, tight to his sides as he stared up.

"Because in that gym, we're all in it together." Nicky gave up on the duvet and accepted he got more warmth from Michael anyway. "You doing all right there?"

"Yeah, it's good," Michael said, but Nicky heard the hesitation in his voice.

"What?"

"Those two mums... you know what they were like." Michael sighed in the semi-darkness, the only light coming from the small lamp next to the bed. "If you hadn't come over and taken control, it would have been...difficult."

Mrs. Milton, Carrie's mum, had caught Michael by the door, and her hands were all over him by the time Nicky had seen it. He'd pulled Michael out, quick as he could, tucking him behind his own body and making things very obvious. It had felt good to do. "Sorry about that. Sorry I didn't get there sooner." He didn't want to think about why it had felt so good.

"You warned me. I'll be more careful next time," Michael said philosophically.

"I'm sorry as well that I had to pet you, kiss you. That was..."

"Better than Mrs. Milton's hand on my dick."

Nicky turned his head on the pillow so he could see Michael properly. "Really? At least she's a woman. It can't be good having a man all over you, especially when you know he's gay. Even if you also know he's acting."

"Why?" Michael asked levelly.

"Because, well, isn't it obvious, with you being straight?"

"I never said I was straight." Michael folded his arms over his chest. "In fact I've never said anything about my sexuality because no one has ever asked me. Never. No one has cared since I set foot in this country."

"Are you straight?" Nicky asked softly.

"Do you care?"

Nicky took him at his word, thinking about it. At the start, Nicky hadn't liked having Michael in his home, in his space. He was a creature of habit. He liked his own company, his routine, and had got annoyed just by knowing that was gone. He liked his books, the quietness, the order, the...but Michael had sort of slipped in and fit easily. Too easily? Maybe he hadn't so much liked his own company as got used to it.

But Michael was more than just a remedy to his solitude. At first Nicky had only let him stay because he couldn't think of an alternative. Now though...yes, he liked Michael, liked the way they got on. Liked talking about his books, sharing them. He liked eating dinner with someone and the easy way they were together. It was so much simpler than he'd ever thought possible.

And he liked Michael now that he said what he thought, expressed an opinion about food, TV, sport, hell, even the books. Michael was intelligent, knew about things he didn't, was informative and articulate. He made Nicky think about stuff, smiled at Nicky's odd habits in a way that wasn't patronizing but was good natured and caring. Nicky thought he would have got on with Michael if they had met in normal circumstances.

He really liked Michael. That was okay, wasn't it?

Sure it was. He liked him as a man, not as a slave. He didn't have to reproach himself for that, surely?

He wasn't so sure that Michael would have given him the time of day though. He knew his life was boring and narrow to most people. But Nicky had long since learned not to care what other people thought of him. He liked his job, his home, his life. He liked Michael and, yes, he did care about him.

"Yes," he said. "I want to know who you are and sex is a part of that."

"I'm bisexual," Michael started before hesitating, briefly. "But, I guess I tried to be straight. My folks wanted it, expected it, and I didn't want to disappoint them, only I probably like men more."

"You couldn't have told them that?"

"They wouldn't have wanted to hear. I tried to say something to my mom a couple of times, but she shut me up real quick. I didn't bother after that. Your parents know and don't mind?"

"The whole world knew I was the queer kid with half a red face." Nicky gave a derisive snort. "As for caring? They never really noticed me, never noticed anything, apart from what was on TV. I don't think they cared one way or the other."

"Cared? Are they dead?" Michael asked.

"They're gone," Nicky said, his voice flat. Then he shook his head briefly, as though to clear that part of the conversation away. "If you're bisexual, does that make it weirder or easier to share a bed like this?"

"I have no idea." Michael laughed. "I expected you to...and when you didn't, I was just grateful, and didn't think about anything else. Now I'm just glad you don't complain about me taking up all the room. Most people I've shared with have."

"You do steal the duvet." Nicky gave an easy laugh as well.

"And you fidget."

"You're like a furnace."

"It makes up for stealing the duvet?"

"Okay, I'll give you that one," Nicky gave in.

It was quiet for a long moment before Nicky reached over and switched off the lamp. The darkness settled comfortably around them, cocooning them in its warmth. When Michael's voice came again, it sounded as unexpected as it was heartfelt. "I feel safer here, in your bed at night, when it's hushed and calm, than I have at any point since this nightmare began. I like it here. I like your teeny-tiny home, where I can almost touch the walls, if I stretch my arms out. I like the random things, the mismatched furniture, the books and the feel of the place. Most of all, I like this bed with you in it."

"I like you being here." And that felt weirder to say than Nicky had imagined.

* * * *

"Stretch through the fingers," Max ordered, demonstrating the move. "Push up through the floor onto your toes, reach out and hold the position. Remember your elegance."

The girls all balanced perfectly, their heads in line with their arms, their faces serene and their postures graceful.

Beth's blush-colored face went even redder as she simultaneously fought to stay in place and impress Max.

Nicky counted the seconds till the agony was over. Elegance? He was pretty sure his elegance was doubled over in the corner laughing its head off at him right now. Then Max called a halt to the suffering and he sagged, knowing life couldn't get any better. But then he looked down at where Michael had collapsed on the floor.

"I'm going to die," Michael whispered in misery.

"It's not that bad."

"The skin between my toes hurts. My hair aches, and everything in between is screaming in protest." Michael rolled onto his back, flopping out. "My arms have gone numb."

"They'll hurt like a bitch when they come back to life," Nicky warned. He offered a hand out to pull Michael up.

"I'm telling you I'm going to die." Michael shook his head at Nicky's hand.

"And I told you ballet is fucking hard work."

"My tongue aches. Why would my tongue ache?"

Just at that moment Adeline came running over, a plastic box in her hand. "Nicky, I..." She stopped, staring at Michael by her feet. "Is he all right?"

Michael gave a pathetic groan and closed his eyes.

"He now has a lot more respect for dancers than he used to have," Nicky said dryly.

"Oh." Adeline smiled. "When he can't walk on Sunday, tell him that he'll feel heaps better after the ballet session on Monday."

There was another groan from the floor, even more pathetic.

"Do you think this might help?" She gave the box to Nicky. "It's a Viennese sponge cake. I haven't made one of those before. It's for you, of course. But should there be any left over..."

Nicky took the box, holding it close to his chest protectively. "I think it might just save his life. But you don't have to make us cakes every week."

"I like making cakes and you—both—like eating them, don't you?"

"Oh yes, eating your cakes is like eating a slice of heaven."

"You're an idiot but I still like you." Adeline beamed at him before running off.

"Come on, home." Nicky pushed at Michael's thigh with his foot.

Michael opened one eye. "Was she lying about Sunday?"

"Nope. The first time I did a ballet workout, I couldn't get up the stairs the day after and on Sunday all I could do was crawl from the bed to the sofa to the bath. But..." He held up the box after lifting the lid and peering inside. "She also wasn't lying about the cake. Out of all the ones she's made us, this looks the best."

"Will it cure me of ballet disease?"

"Judging by the amount you love cake, I think it'll cure you of just about anything. I hate the fact you don't get fat." This time when Nicky held out his hand, Michael used it to pull himself up.

"Does your hatred mean I'm not getting out of ballet training?"

"Too fucking right it does." Nicky laughed. "It's good for you. Now let's go and try to stop Beth blushing as Max leaves, and console her over a few beers because he'll never return her undying love."

"I would, but my legs don't work," Michael said.

"You'll live." Nicky threw a sympathetic arm around his shoulders and pulled him in the direction of the showers.

* * * *

Nicky took a step back trying to see the asymmetric bars movement from another angle. It was wrong. Something was wrong, off, but he couldn't work out what it was. Carrie was trying the Tkachev, a move she knew well. She could perform it capably on a single bar, but now they were putting it in the middle of her bar routine, and they needed it to fit, so she caught hold between the high and low bar.

She'd hit the bottom bar once, and now her confidence had gone. She was making a mistake, but

Nicky couldn't work out what it was. The trouble was that he had to stand behind the lower bar to push her forward, if needed, if she looked like she was going to hit it. He couldn't see properly from there.

He looked round the gym. Everyone was working – Beth was deeply involved in mapping out spacing on the floor for an acrobatic pass, and there was no one else strong and big enough. Then he saw Michael, who was sorting out hand chalk. "Hey," he called out. "Would you mind helping me?"

"What's up?" Michael came over.

"I need someone to stand here and give Carrie a little push forward if it seems like she's too close to the lower bar and might hit it." Nicky explained the problem and why he needed to be somewhere else. He got her to demonstrate the move again, showing Michael just where to stand and what to do. "We've had a mat over the bottom bar but she needs the confidence to do it without that. Don't touch her unless she's going to knock it. In fact…" He grinned at Carrie. "She's so good you won't have to do anything, but it helps just to know someone is there. Doesn't it, sweetheart?"

Carrie stared hard at Michael. "Let me see your hands? I need to know they're big enough."

Michael held his palms out, fingers spread. "They're really big, really strong. I won't let you get hurt, trust me."

She gave him a hard, uncompromising look, then nodded. "I trust you," she said, and went to re-chalk her hands.

Nicky gave Michael a short, tight grin then they went through the move again, with Nicky standing at the side. "Got it," he said, already pulling up a huge box so he could reach her mid-flight. Michael automatically went to help, then he went back to stand behind the lower bar.

Half an hour later Nicky was rubbing Carrie's hands and grinning hugely. "We nailed it, sweetpea. No, you nailed it. The inward Tkachev is yours. You tamed its miserable, complaining arse. You smacked it into next week."

She looked up at him, grinning just as widely. "It's a good thing you're an amazing coach, because you do talk a lot of nonsense."

"Well, it's just as well you're an amazing gymnast then. You did good, girl, you really did."

The grin slipped from her face, leaving it open and needy. "Really?" she asked.

"Really," he said. "Now go get a drink before we do something else, something that'll give your hands a rest."

He started to put the equipment back in its place as Michael helped. "You did good, as well," Nicky said. "The girls don't usually take to someone new. For her to trust you is a big deal."

"It's you," Michael said. "I've said it before. You set the tone in this place and it's...great." He smiled, soft, small and just for Nicky. "Sorry, I can't come up with a better word. I like the way you keep the rest of the world out, and everyone here is equal — the older girls and the ones still working their way up. I like working here."

"Want to help with more of the coaching?" Nicky asked.

"Am I allowed to?"

"Not really, because you're not qualified. But we can always use another intelligent pair of eyes and a strong pair of hands. With Beth or I supervising, you'll be fine."

"And Pattinson, the mums?"

"Won't care if we get results."

"Then I'd like that, I really would."

"Good. We'll stick you at the front for the next ballet training. It won't help you coach, but it will make the girls laugh."

* * * *

On Sunday afternoon they sat, squashed onto the sofa, as Nicky talked through the routine they were watching on video. He knew he was being too technical, that Michael didn't know what half the things he said meant, but he couldn't stop himself. He loved the grace of gymnastics, the artistry of a simple move performed perfectly, but he also loved this — dissecting a move till he knew how it worked.

He was also full up, mellow from a lunchtime beer, relaxed and truly comfortable. Why shouldn't he indulge himself? There was even some of Adeline's latest cake left.

"So she has to lift her hips at that point?" Michael asked, pointing at the TV screen.

"More than just her hips. She has to make sure her whole center of gravity is high enough so she has time to complete the move before she lands."

"What was this? I mean, who is it?"

"She's Chinese. Retired now but one of the best. This is the World Championship, from about nine years ago."

"This is the World Championship?" Michael eyebrows rose. "But, I don't get it. You must have three girls as good as that. More that will be eventually."

"Yep," Nicky said brightly. "I know how to pick them."

"But...are you really that good a coach?"

"Yes." Nicky was certain. "I know the technical side, know how to get them to want to work and I believe in style, not just difficulty."

"So you've had others in the past that have done really well?"

Nicky huffed, less enthusiastic now. "I had a couple of girls that could have been really good, the best, but it didn't happen."

"Why not?" Michael passed over the bowl of popcorn.

"Because." Again Nicky huffed, then squared his shoulders and went on. "Because it became obvious to the national governing body just how good they were, and they were taken away from me."

"Why?"

"They were sent to the elite school. It was thought they needed better than the moldy old gym we work in." It was true, Nicky's gym was moldy in the corners, shabby in the rest. It lacked the high tech equipment many had, but he had everything he needed. He was confident in that.

"What happened to them?" Michael asked.

"They lost their way, stopped being so good." Nicky pushed the bowl back. "Let's say they didn't take to the new regime. They didn't like being shouted at."

"I can imagine why." Michael took more popcorn, eating it while he thought, and the girl on the TV got her score to rapturous applause. "So will they do that again? Take away Adeline and Martha? Those two are as good as any of those." He pointed at the screen again.

"I hope not. They'd only go the same way. Luckily, I think the powers that be know that."

"But..." Michael stopped, appearing to think it through. "I don't get it. If you're that good, why don't they support you properly? They should give you a decent place to work, extra staff. Hell, they should pay you a salary you can live on."

"I don't care about any of that." Nicky dismissed it.

"You might not care, but you're a huge asset. They should support you. Instead you have Pattinson on your back and you're scraping around for money. That can't be right." Michael frowned.

Nicky sighed and muted the TV. The girl in the picture danced along to silence. "You have to understand some things about me," he said quietly. "I have...history. One that makes the government treat me in a certain way."

Michael licked the sticky popcorn from his lips before looking over at Nicky. "Did you do something?"

"No, I didn't. But my parents did," Nicky admitted. He knew he had to explain things properly to Michael — that he should have done it before now, but it would be the first time he'd said it out loud. Even Beth had already known most of the story and he'd only had to add in the details. This was different.

"What happened? Michael asked.

"My parents were..." How did he explain anything? "They were old, ordinary, boring. I'm their only child and I always knew they were...when I was a kid they seemed so gray that no one noticed them. They blended into the background so you couldn't even see them — they were that unremarkable. The only notable thing about them was the fact they had a gay son with a birthmark on his face. But they pretty much ignored all that, and me, so it didn't really matter."

He leaned his head back, gazing up at the ceiling, remembering back across the years. It wasn't a pleasant thing to do. "When I was nineteen, I was training at a sports center, failing at being a gymnast."

"Failing? You?" Michael said, sounding surprised.

"Yes. I had the content and the style but I buckled under pressure. Routines that were fantastic in training crumbled in competition. I didn't have the nerve for the big time, or any time really. I was fighting to prove something, to myself as much as anyone, when my mum rang me. She said they were going away for a little bit the next day, and asked if I wanted to go. I tried to explain what was happening with me but, as usual, she wasn't listening." He stopped for a moment, trying to explain things properly. He had the benefit of hindsight and it felt important that he got it right. Got it right for Michael.

"Turns out 'going away for a little bit' meant they were making a run for it. They worked in low level admin jobs but they'd been stealing from the government for years. Had stolen a fortune and no one had even noticed because they were so bland."

"My God." Michael sucked in a breath. "They stole from the government here? That's…"

"Yeah, it is, isn't it?" Nicky said, ruefully. "First I knew about it was when I was hauled out of the gym, in front of everyone, by armed police."

"Shit, what happened?"

"They kept me locked up for days, questioned me for hours but I didn't know a damned thing. Eventually I was let out but everything was gone. There was no place for me at the center anymore, my parents' house had been ripped apart. I had nowhere to go." He pressed his lips together and straightened his neck, turning to look at Michael. "It's no sob story. I ended up coaching, which I love, and I'm good at. But it does mean the government isn't on my side. They don't trust me."

"Why not? You didn't do anything. Didn't they get their pound of flesh from your parents?"

"I have no idea," Nicky admitted. "I don't know if the government caught them or if they got out of the country somehow. I've never heard a word from them or about them since that day."

"You don't know if they're alive?"

"No," Nicky said simply. "But I do know I've never been flavor of the month since then. If I didn't get good results with the girls, there's no way I'd be in charge. They aren't going to turn my success down, they want to win on a world stage, but they aren't going to do much to help."

"So you put up with shit conditions and lousy pay for something you didn't do?"

"There's nothing I can do about it. They want to take it out on someone." Nicky shrugged. "But I'm doing what I love. Plus—and it's a big plus—they leave me alone to do it. I'm happy with that."

"But it doesn't seem right, doesn't seem fair," Michael persisted.

"And having slaves is fair?"

"No, but that's different."

"Worse."

"Okay, worse. But what they're doing to you is still wrong."

Again Nicky shrugged, this time not so helpless, more accepting. "It's helped make me who I am." He twisted right round on the small sofa so he could face Michael. "I've been scared, really scared. Maybe not as scared as you but, when I saw it on your face, I had to do whatever I could to stop it."

"Well, I appreciate that. Not that you've been scared, no, not that at all," Michael hastened to add. "But that you're prepared to put yourself out to prevent it where you can."

"I hope what happened to me has made me a better man. But I'll be honest, at first I didn't want to put myself out all that much," Nicky admitted. "I figured Beth and I would come up with some way of keeping you safe without you having to live with me for so long."

"I'm sorry." Michael looked away. "Sorry I'm still here."

"Hey, no, I didn't mean that. I was making a crack about how useless we are, that months down the line we're no closer to a plan than we were at the start." Nicky caught hold of Michael's sleeve and pulled. "I like having you here. You stop me being so…weird." Should that have been hard to say? No, it was okay to like Michael, surely?

"You're not weird," Michael said, his attention back on Nicky. "You've had shit thrown at you your whole life and yet you're still in the game, still fighting, still working for something you love. What's a few books and a mountain of videos compared to that?"

"You know what?" Nicky reached across for more popcorn. "You've caught weird disease from me. You have it almost as bad."

* * * *

Nicky thought about his plan long and hard. It seemed a nice idea, he thought it would be appreciated, but he didn't know what to actually do.

In the end he decided to keep it simple, keep it safe. After all, safe was the most important thing and, he didn't have much money, so simple was probably a prerequisite.

It was Michael's birthday—a fact he'd found out when he'd been putting Michael's papers in a safe place.

It was Michael's birthday and Michael had had a shitty time, so it seemed like a good idea to do something nice for him. He wanted to make him smile. He liked watching Michael smile. But what could he do?

He'd thought about a party at the gym but that was putting the girls at risk. It was one thing for them to accept Michael, to talk to him and treat him like the other adults they worked with. But it was quite another for them to celebrate his birthday. Michael was a slave—slaves didn't have lives, weren't supposed to be treated as people. The girls knew enough to treat him one way when they were all alone, another when there was anyone else around. They were even careful when it was time to go home and the mums were there.

No, he couldn't ask the girls to lie, and they would certainly have to for a slave's birthday party.

Even a party at home wouldn't be easy. If someone saw, an outsider, then there could, no, would be trouble. Nicky knew the rules.

So instead he'd arranged a little 'impromptu gathering'. Beth, himself and Miss F from downstairs. Not a great line up, he'd admit, but Miss F was very taken with Michael. It had become her mission in life to take care of him, and that meant everything from stopping unexpected visitors to making sure he ate right.

It was surprising how many people wanted to check up on Michael's eating habits. Adeline still made him a cake every Friday, although it was always, technically, given to Nicky. But it was Michael's opinion on it she sought out on Saturday morning. Which was why Nicky had given a not so subtle hint about birthdays a week before.

Adeline didn't fail him, just like he knew she wouldn't. "Oh," she said, Friday morning, as innocent as a newborn. "I was bored so I made a bigger cake this week. It's nothing special." She handed over a huge plastic box and Nicky had to brace himself to take the weight.

Inside was a two-tiered birthday cake with piped blue flowers, icing, chocolate buttons stuck all over it and candles. She'd even added candles. "You might want to put it in the fridge," she said, as though butter wouldn't melt in her mouth.

"What did you tell your mum?" Nicky asked.

"That I was experimenting, of course. But she's not silly. She taught me how to make the flowers," she added, nonchalantly. "I hope...people enjoy it, and before you ask, no, I won't say a word." Then she ran off to join the warm up.

Nicky grinned. Now he had a cake, a homemade card that didn't say 'birthday' on it anywhere so no one could object and a bottle of whiskey wrapped up in Christmas paper. It had been on sale, dirt cheap, and no one looked at the paper anyway. He drew a silly face—he thought it was a pig sticking its tongue out, but he wasn't sure. He wasn't that good at drawing—cut it out and glued it on the top. Then added hands, or paws.

If it made him smile he hoped it would do the same for Michael.

That night Michael soaked in the bath just as Nicky knew he would. Ballet training was hard, and it didn't get easier for at least a few months. Michael had a couple of weeks to go.

"My armpits ache." Michael moaned from the bedroom as he got dressed afterwards. "Why on earth do my armpits ache? I hate ballet. I'm telling you, that Max is a sadist who just wants to see this grown man cry. He got close to it today. I nearly howled like a baby, and I..." He stopped in the doorway to the living room, still rubbing at his damp hair with a towel. "What the...?"

They stood in a faintly pitiable semi-circle, glasses held aloft amid choruses of 'happy birthday'. Miss F had made a banner especially. But again, she'd had to be careful. It said 'Happy Special Day' in blue felt tip pen, her spidery writing getting smaller as she fought for space to get in the last word.

But it was a banner for Michael, to celebrate his birthday. He inhaled hard, holding it as his gaze went from one to the next. "Thank you," he said, voice thick with emotion. "Thank you all so much, it means a lot that..." And then his words threatened to splinter and break and everyone rushed to fill the gap.

"I got you a card," Nicky said. "Well, technically I had to make it but, hey, the thought was there."

"I bought a card," Beth one-upped him. "It may say 'Happy Mother's Day' but I figured that would just confuse anyone who came nosing around."

"I have a present for you." Miss F thrust a small parcel into his hand. It was wrapped in paper with tiny flowers all over it and at least half a roll of sticky tape. "It's bath salts, for your aching muscles. I know how you suffer. I picked lavender especially. Such a fragrant flower, don't you think?"

"I think it's fuc...it's completely wonderful," Michael said effusively, then kissed her on the cheek. Her blush seemed to go in and out of the deep wrinkles on her face. "I think you're all completely wonderful."

"Here." Nicky handed over his present.

Michael's grin grew even wider as he saw the packaging. "A cat?"

"Hell, it's meant to be a pig. I think." Nicky made a face of mock annoyance before hugging Michael briefly and patting him on the back.

Beth held out her offering. "You tell the girls I gave you this and I'll kick you in the balls," she announced.

Michael took it, ripped off the paper then started laughing so hard his damp hair danced around his face. Inside the box were piles of sweets and chocolates. All things the girls weren't allowed. "This has to be one of the best birthdays ever," Michael said.

"Really?" Nicky looked at him closely, then shook his head. "It gets better. Wait till you see what Adeline did for you."

When he came back into the living room, Beth had switched off the lights and closed the curtains. The candles on the cake lit up the room and Michael's face.

"Thank you," Michael whispered. "Just...thank you. This couldn't get any better."

And just like it had been planned by an evil director of a second rate movie, it was right at that moment that someone knocked at the front door.

"Wait here," Nicky said, suddenly serious. He shut them all in the living room and took a deep breath before going to find out who it was.

Adeline stood on the step, her mother just behind her. "I saw Beth's card," she said straight faced. "And we thought, if it's Mother's Day, you'd need more than a cake to celebrate. So we made sausage rolls, cheese straws, a dip thing that doesn't look quite right to me and lots more. Are you going to invite us in?"

"But I...you shouldn't...it's dangerous..." Nicky tried.

Adeline tsk'ed and pushed past him, her arms full of plastic boxes. "Don't worry," her mother said softly, holding Nicky's arm. "I parked my car right across the bottom of the steps. No one can get up here without my moving it. Now, are you sure you want us? Adeline said, but I wasn't so sure."

"Yes," Nicky said decisively, dragging her in. "Yes, I'm really, really sure I want you both."

As he locked the front door and threw the bolts, Adeline called out. "This isn't a proper party without music. Nicky, haven't you got any?"

"And no, we don't want a book about it," Beth added, laughing.

* * * *

That night, in bed, Michael turned on his side and tried to thank Nicky yet again.

"Shut up," Nicky insisted. "You said it enough already. It wasn't a big deal."

"It was a fucking awesome birthday." Michael was firm. His voice wasn't slurred but it was soft around the edges, mellow. "One I'll remember forever."

"I suppose you're bound to remember your first birthday as a slave."

"Don't put a downer on it, man. Watching Miss F get drunk and tell dirty stories was pretty memorable. So was hearing Beth go on about her never ending love for Max. But a birthday surrounded by real friends," Michael said simply. "That's pretty awesome." He touched Nicky's shoulder lightly. "You did all that, so thank you. Thank you for bringing light to the darkness."

"Light to the darkness?" Nicky pulled a face at him. "You're either as drunk as Miss F or you've read too many of my books." He patted the back of Michael's hand easily. "Go to sleep before you profess never ending love for your lavender bath salts."

Chapter Five

"And again," Nicky said firmly. "No, you can't lose your style, your grace, just because the move is hard or you're tired. Try it again."

Adeline's shoulders slumped, her back rounding. But she was made of stern stuff and her iron will had gotten her this far. She wouldn't allow it to let her down now. She blew out a long breath, deliberately stood as tall and straight as she could, and repeated the double pirouette on the end of the beam. This time her free leg was held high and straight, her head kept at an angle that made her look elegant and untouchable.

"Well?" she asked, finishing the move with precision.

"Better. Not as sharp as I've seen you do it, but not bad for the end of a long session like this."

Adeline nodded her acceptance.

"But you have to do it that well every time, no exceptions," Nicky insisted.

"You want me to do it again?"

"No. Now we'll move on to the dismount."

It had been a hard session but it wasn't over yet, at least not for the four oldest girls. The others had gone home an hour ago, partly because it was the normal finishing time but mostly because all the coaching was focused elsewhere.

Work in the gym had been like that for the last three weeks and it would continue for another six days. Endless sessions that covered every piece of equipment, focused on perfecting routines that were already as good as they could make them. But no one was going to take a chance, leave anything untried, unworked.

In six days' time the National Championships started. They would be held in a huge new auditorium on the other side of the country. Not only would it be televised but also the selectors for the World Championships would be watching. They'd be watching very, very closely.

This was so important everyone could taste it in the air.

This was the first step to competing with the very best in the world. To beating the very best in the world.

The girls knew it and now everything was focused on that goal. They no longer danced around, happy and carefree, laughing and joking together. Now no movement was wasted, no risk taken, no injury could be tolerated. Now they concentrated hard, thinking through the slightest hand movement, stretching through every toe. Concentrating hard to make everything perfect but with the grace and style that was their trademark.

They would be ready, they were ready. If one of them didn't win it wouldn't be for lack of effort, from gymnasts and coaches alike.

That night, after the session finished, Nicky seriously considered holding onto Michael's waistband so he would be dragged up the stairs as they reached home. He wasn't so much physically tired as emotionally. He had three girls going to the Nationals — one was a bit of a wild card but two most certainly had a realistic chance of winning. Two.

That meant, even if everything went as well as it could, one wouldn't win. He was perfectly aware they'd think coming second was failure, no matter how much they adored their gym-mate.

One of his girls wouldn't win, maybe both. Adeline's grace or Martha's technical brilliance?

Once more he thanked the powers that be that he didn't have to decide.

"Come on, old man." Michael turned round and gave him a weary smile before grabbing his jacket sleeve and pulling him up the last few steps. "Home, food, bed. In that order."

Nicky nodded and let himself be dragged.

By the day before they were due to leave for the competition, nervous exhaustion had given way to fever pitch excitement tempered by nerves. Nicky wrote endless lists of things for the girls to remember then crossed most out, saying it would be overload. In the end he sat them down in the middle of the floor area and went over the mental strategies they'd practiced. Focusing skills, others to block out the rest of the arena and the audience. So many things needed for a high level event like this one.

At last he sat back and smiled at all three. "Remember," he said. "You do gymnastics because you love it. Enjoy the competition and don't worry about anyone else. As long as you do your best, you can be proud of yourselves. That's all that matters."

"And making you proud of us," Adeline said softly.

"Sweetpea." This time Nicky's smile was more heartfelt. "If you fall over and twist your ankle going up for your first apparatus, I'll still be proud of you." He looked round at them all. "I couldn't be more proud to work with such amazing people as you. Now, go home and sleep well. You're going to need it."

Then he made his own way home.

After dinner, Michael started to clear up, and Nicky automatically began helping. "Don't bother." Michael took the plate from him. "I'll do this while you go and pack. You all have an early start for the airport tomorrow."

Nicky relinquished the plate but picked up another, turning his back on Michael as he put it in the sink. "I don't have to pack."

"Why not? You can't do it in the morning, there won't be time."

It was silent for a long time till Nicky twisted round, leaning back against the counter and briefly closing his eyes. Then he turned his full attention on Michael. "I don't have to pack, because I'm not going."

"What?" Michael's eyes rounded, and his mouth opened wide "You have to go, the girls are relying on you. They need you."

"They'll have Beth." Nicky tried to shrug but it came out half-hearted at best.

"Beth's good, but you're their coach. You're the one they respect, the one they go to after every routine, the one they lean on for everything. You can't let them down."

"They'll be okay with her. They'll understand."

"Understand?" Again Michael's eyes widened some more as he dropped the plate back down on the table.

"Why would they do that when I don't? You've all worked for years to get to this point, why in God's name would you let them down now?"

"Because I can't go," Nicky said level and simple.

"Why not? Has the governing body banned you? Are they trying to push you out again?"

"No, it's not them."

"Then what?" Michael demanded.

"I can't go because I can't leave you." And it really was as simple as that.

"Me?" Michael took a step back. "What have I got to do with anything?"

"I can't take you with me, but I can't leave you, not on your own, not for days."

"But..." Michael said. "I'll just stay here. I won't open the door, won't go out. I'll be okay."

"Too many people know you'll be here alone. Miss F won't be able to protect you, only I can do that."

"No." Michael shook his head hard. "I'm not spoiling everything for the girls. I won't turn the lights on. I'll stay real quiet. No one will know I'm here. They'll all think you left me somewhere else."

"Everyone knows I don't have 'somewhere else'. Just like they'll know you're here." Nicky didn't move from his position against the counter. There was nothing else to do. Nowhere to go and nothing to do.

"But you always said if I don't open the door, I'm okay."

"If anyone tried anything, Miss F would ring me at work and I could be back in a few minutes," he explained. "This time I'd be the other side of the country. I wouldn't be able to get to you, not from there. All they have to do is say they saw someone trying to break in and the authorities would open the door to check. I'm pretty sure the police would join in and enjoy themselves with you."

"But..." There was fear on Michael's face now, but also fierce determination to honor his loyalty to the girls. "Who would do that? Pattinson? He's a bit creepy but not that bad."

"I'm guessing 'not that bad' doesn't mean you want to be forced to have sex with him." Nicky crossed his arms over his chest, sure of his ground.

"No, I don't. But his mum would have him by the balls if he did. She owns the gym, and she adores you. You also put on a really good act of being in love with me. She fell for it, she won't let him hurt what you love."

"Are you really willing to risk it? Even if you are, if it's not him, it would be someone else."

"Who? Who else is there that knows or cares about me?" Michael's anger at the situation, the world, was obviously rising along with his confusion.

"Fuck it, Michael. You're not that naive." Nicky's frustration wasn't that far behind. "The guy who came to fix the heater at the gym, the one that works on the checkout at the supermarket, the man who delivers the bottled water. They've all seen you, seen your slave T-shirt, licked their lips and thought about it. Way too many people know about you and know about the championship. Beth and I talked it through and, although she doesn't like it, we agreed that there's no other option."

"You talked to Beth and not me?"

"It's my problem, not yours." And that really was the truth. Michael was his responsibility, his problem.

"Your problem?" Michael put so much emphasis on the first word it was in danger of caving in on itself.

"Your arse, my problem." Nicky started collecting things up again. As far as he was concerned, this argument was over. There was nothing left to say. Neither of them might like it but there was no other alternative.

"That's fucking stupid." Michael spat the words out. He stood between the table and the sink, feet spread wide, hands on hips, face contorted up with all kinds of things. "Have you told the girls? They're going to be devastated."

"No, I haven't done it yet. I'll call them when they get there. But they'll understand."

"Are you sure? Adeline is going to cry her heart out."

"Yes, she probably will, and she won't be right all through the competition." Nicky stopped moving, staring hard at Michael. He'd had a long time to think about this, Michael hadn't. Only time didn't make anything any easier. "But she was the one that first asked what arrangements I'd made for you."

"You can't do that to her, not because of me. She needs you."

"She'll understand. She'd expect it of me."

"But you're ruining their chances. After all that work, all that effort, you're throwing everything away before they even start," Michael said, desperation in his voice, knowing it was his fault.

"I have no choice." He knew Michael was right, knew he was letting his girls down, but what else could he do? The knowledge didn't stop it ripping a hole in his heart, though.

"I don't know how you can do it. You love those girls." Michael shook his head, disappointment in Nicky clear on his face.

"I do love them," Nicky said, the thought making the hole wider, deeper. Making it hurt even more and leaving him in shreds. "Only I love you more." The words slipped out without thought or reflection. He knew he'd had no intention of saying anything like that.

Where had it come from? Why had he said it?

Did he mean it?

As soon as the words were free, he closed up tight. Those were words that shouldn't be said. Every atom in his body was screaming at him about the huge mistake he'd made.

Of course he meant it.

He might not have thought about it, might not have admitted it to himself, not even at three in the morning when he was feeling at his most vulnerable and pathetic. But, as soon as the words had taken shape and become a concrete reality, that he couldn't ignore, he knew he meant them.

He wanted to turn back time, to erase those five simple-sounding words. To hide, to run.

As the atmosphere in the room seemed to shimmer and hold its breath and Michael stared at him, he quickly grabbed up the last cutlery, throwing it in the vague direction of the sink before he stalked out of the room. "I'm going for a shower."

If he couldn't take the words back, he could get away from them.

"Nicky?" Michael paused for a long, long beat before going after him. "Did you mean that?"

"No, of course I didn't mean it." Nicky stopped in the hallway. It might just have been a lie but it was one that needed to be said and had to be believed. Had to be. "I'm just worried about you."

"You did mean it," Michael stated, awed. "You love me."

"And now you sound like a kid in the playground." Nicky tried to turn away again. Was nothing going to go right for him?

"Don't do that." Michael stopped him again, his words pinning Nicky in place. "Don't you dismiss it like it's nothing. It is true and it's important."

"So what if it is true?" No, nothing was going to go easy. He couldn't even hide it or deny it, he was that stupid. Now, he knew, he sounded weary beyond reason. "It doesn't matter. I'd protect you, no matter what."

"You love me, and it doesn't matter?"

"Michael." Nicky sighed hard, pressing a hand against the wall as though it were the only thing holding him up. "I'm sorry, I wish it hadn't slipped out, because it'll only complicate things. But it really doesn't matter. However I feel doesn't mean anything has to change. We just carry on as we are."

"But you love me?"

"Stop saying it, you sound like an idiot. You make me sound like an idiot." Nicky ran a hand through his hair, down over his face, then glanced around thinking there must be somewhere he could run away to. "Can't we just pretend it never happened?"

"Why? Why can't I know?" Michael's sheer size blocked the door to the kitchen, fixing Nicky in place.

"Oh for the love of all things sane," Nicky burst out, shaking his head. "Think about it. I own you, I keep you safe, and now I say I love you? I don't want you feeling obliged to do anything you don't want to. I'm not a charity case."

"And what if I do want to?" Michael asked, tongue pressed against the front of his top teeth.

"See." Nicky's face flushed with anger. "That's exactly what I didn't want to happen. You don't have to keep me sweet. I'm going to protect you, no matter what. You don't have to sleep with me to get me to do it."

"I already sleep with you." Michael snorted. "What if I want to have sex with you?"

Nicky shook his head. "You didn't half an hour ago. Why should you now? Only reason is because you feel the pressure of those three little words."

"Who says I didn't want to half an hour ago?" Michael demanded, pushing into Nicky's space, intimidating.

"No, enough. I've had enough of this conversation." Nicky made it to the living room this time, before Michael cornered him again between the bookshelf and the TV.

"You don't want to have this conversation, so we don't? What about what I want?"

"Jesus." Nicky hissed. "I'm meant to be your owner. At least let me pretend I act like one at times. I don't want this conversation. Don't castrate me further by taking away my right not to talk."

"I don't castrate you," Michael exclaimed, affronted.

"No, okay, that was harsh," Nicky conceded. "But I have given you just about everything I've got, from my home and food to my last penny, my secrets and even my reputation."

"Your reputation?" Michael said. "What did I do to that?"

Now Nicky was bristling. Nothing ever went easy for him, nothing was ever simple. But it had been easy and simple and good with Michael. Only, instead of counting his blessings, he'd gone and ruined it by opening his mouth. He thought he'd have more sense, but now he couldn't seem to stop talking. And there was Michael, standing all big and strong and beautiful and not understanding. Well, maybe he should make him.

"Have you any idea how many times I get the word muppet thrown at me? I knew it was going to be bad but it was even written on the back of my sweatshirt last week. That and the looks, the questions about how often I bend over for you, the comments about knowing the girls are safe in my care. People laugh in my face but I take it, take it happily, because it protects you. I do it because you're my friend, not because I love you. So I don't need you saying stuff you don't mean. You already have everything I've got, leave me a little self-respect."

"What the hell?" Michael sounded confused. "I didn't know it was that bad, didn't know you felt like that. But I'd certainly never do anything to damage your self-respect."

"Then stop implying you want sex," Nicky said simply.

"I'm not implying it, I'm saying it out loud, I want sex with you. But I don't understand how that affects your self-respect." Michael took a step closer, and Nicky instantly took one of his own, farther away.

"Because I've had it drummed into me that people like you don't have sex with people like me unless they feel sorry for them, owe them or it's an obligation."

"What?" Now Michael looked incredulous, his eyes stretched wide, his face shocked. "That is so screwed up as to be insane. Who are 'people like you' and 'people like me'?"

Nicky sighed, the sound and sentiment seeming to come from his gut, his very soul. He shook his head.

He was tired, so tired of all the things he couldn't control. "Look at you," he said and sank into an armchair. "You're young, good-looking, confident, intelligent, thoughtful, kind and so far out of my league as to be on another planet."

"How can you say that? I'm only a bit younger than you, and you're…beautiful."

Nicky lifted his chin, his gaze focused on Michael. "I might only be a few years older, but sometimes I feel about a hundred. I've had shit happen to me for so long that I must be magnet for the stuff or I deserve it. I'm the gay kid with half a red face, the one that didn't have the balls to make it as a gymnast. Even my own, sadder still parents didn't want me, and my government is suspicious of me and treats me like scum. No wonder most people dismiss me as nothing. So from down here, I can't even see the league you're in."

"None of that is true," Michael said, shaking his head. "None of it."

"It's all true. That's how everyone here sees me," Nicky said. "I've been slapped down so hard and so often that it's the position I'm forced into, and there's fuck all I can do about it. But I deal with everything and say a silent, 'screw you', to the world, just…" He waved a hand around ineffectually. "Just don't start being nice to me by saying you want sex. I don't need your pity or anything else. I know who I am, what I am, the ways in which I'm strong, and I don't want your sympathy." He went on, confident now, sure of his ground. "As you've certainly worked out by now I don't have much of a sex life. That's because I don't like casual much, and I suck at proper relationships. I'm also not great at making new friends. Right now I think of you as a friend, and that's more important to me than sex. So please, forget what I said and let's be friends?"

"I...we are, but..."

"No, no buts. Friends?"

"Of course I'm your friend, but..."

"Please," Nicky interrupted again, knowing he sounded at the end of the line. "Just leave it. I can't do this, not now. I'm tired and I want to go to bed. I have enough to handle with the girls. I don't need anything else."

"Nicky," Michael said again but Nicky couldn't take anymore. He heaved himself up, walked away then forced the bathroom door shut and locked it securely behind him. Just before he turned on the shower, Nicky thought he heard a huff of annoyance from the other side of the door. He ignored it and got into the hot water.

* * * *

Later that night, as Nicky lay side by side with Michael in bed, he was aware that they were both staring up at the ceiling, both wide awake.

"This is weird," Michael said, eventually. "Everything feels different. We feel different. What are we going to do now?"

"What do you want to do?" Nicky asked, and even he could hear the hesitancy in his voice.

"Well, we could have sex? It's been a long time for both of us."

"And that's it?" Nicky shook his head. "That's your reason for us having sex? That's all you've got?"

"It's a pretty good reason. Plus" — Michael started counting things off on his fingers — "you're also damned beautiful, a truly decent person and..."

"Shut up." Nicky wasn't joking. "That's not good enough."

"Why not?"

Nicky sighed, the sound just a little desperate. "Like I said, I'm not great at casual, but I can do it if I don't have to see the person again. I can even do repeat performances if that's all there is, just sex. What I can't do is casual with a friend. I can't handle that."

"But we're more than friends. We're—"

"Michael," Nicky interrupted. "Don't say stuff you don't mean."

"I'm very fond of you. I could—"

"I'm not surprised," Nicky interrupted again. "Of course you're 'fond' of me, I'm the one that protects your arse, you're bound to be fond of me. But it doesn't mean anything." He looked over briefly, his gaze never quite meeting Michael's. "But you're not in love with me, and it would screw things up too much if we started fucking. Now we work because we're friends. Don't mess with something that works." With that he turned on his side, his back to Michael.

"But I am very fond of you," Michael said softly, into the darkness.

"Then be nice to me. I have to talk to the girls tomorrow, tell them what's going on. Cut me some slack and leave things alone."

There was a long moment of silence, then Michael reached over and squeezed Nicky's shoulder before turning on his side and going to sleep.

Nicky had told Adeline that sex was about two people caring and sharing, and he meant it.

* * * *

Next morning Nicky sat outside on the step, the phone pressed to his ear, when Michael brought him out a cup of coffee. He was back there again numerous times throughout the day, talking to all three girls and Beth. They were upset but they understood, he informed Michael at lunch time, before the subject was firmly closed again.

They had to understand – the National Championships started the next day.

The following morning Nicky went into the gym, worked with those girls who had been left behind then went home to watch the competition, live on the television. Before it started, Nicky sat outside talking animatedly to the girls. Then he had to hang up. There was nothing more he could do, nothing he could say.

From the first sight of them on TV, it was obvious things weren't right, they weren't right. Nicky could see Beth in the background of one shot talking to Adeline, her face cupped between Beth's hands. Nicky knew what she'd be saying. 'Do it for Nicky, make him proud.' And Adeline gave her all.

They sat watching all afternoon – the usual second training session had been canceled. The sandwich Michael brought Nicky was left ignored till it dried and curled on the plate.

When Adeline fell from the beam, it wasn't on the complicated acrobatic pass or even the dismount. It was a simple leap she'd done a million times before. The fall even had her trademark style and grace but it was still a fall.

Her fight for the medals was over.

Michael tried to say something but Nicky simply got up and walked away, thankful that Michael wasn't stupid enough to try to follow him.

Martha's problems weren't anything like as obvious. She made all her moves but the precision wasn't there. The ease and confidence had gone.

The girls sat, heads down, on either side of Beth, and didn't watch the rest of the competition.

They finished with Martha in fourth place, Adeline in eighth. Lily, the wild card third gymnast who'd just gone for the experience, made seventh, which was a surprise to everyone.

That evening Nicky sat on the bed talking to the girls for hours. There was little he could say other than to tell them how proud he was of them then try to boost their confidence for the individual apparatus events that were still to come over the next two days.

Adeline won a gold on the floor, Martha gold on bars. Those were expected, it would have been shocking if they didn't win, but neither made up for the disappointment of the overall competition.

Michael tried to talk to Nicky, to apologize or commiserate, to break the pressure, but Nicky didn't want to hear. On Michael's fifth or sixth attempt— stumbled words of regret as he stood in the bathroom doorway—Nicky pushed past him, away. But then he stopped, looking back. He saw his own face in the bathroom mirror, it was tight and bleak. "This isn't about you, not now," he said.

"Okay. But if it isn't, can we talk about the other great cloud that's hanging over us?" Michael tried again. "You're acting like it's a bad thing, like you made some great mistake, but you didn't. You like me, I like you—why can't we find some happiness, get some pleasure together?"

Nicky's face tightened even further as his fingers tensed on the wall. "Don't you get it? Now is about those girls, my girls. Everything is about them, it always has been. It has to be."

"But…"

"No." Nicky wouldn't listen to anymore. He turned his back and walked away. He might love Michael but now was all about his girls.

Despite the warmth of the duvet and Michael's furnace-like qualities, the room felt cold that night as they lay in bed.

When the girls arrived back at the gym the following day, Nicky was already waiting for them. Martha ran over to him, throwing her arms around his chest, burying her cheek against him. Lily wasn't far behind. But Adeline hesitated by the door, her eyes huge and dark in her pale face.

Eventually Nicky let go of the other girls and gazed over to her. Then he fell to his knees and held out his arms to her. She ran, faster than he'd ever seen her go before, gripping hold of him and holding her breath as she pressed in tight. He gathered them all close—a bubble from which all else were barred.

For the next hour they sat on a pile of mats in the corner, whispering frenetically, whilst everyone else worked around them. When Nicky finally led them down, they were all smiling and still holding onto each other.

Michael came over to them and tried to apologize to the girls but Martha waved his attempts away. "It's nothing you did," she said confidently. "We'll work things out with Nicky. We always work things out with him." She straightened her back, eyes wide and honest. "We might not have won but that doesn't matter. Nicky is proud of us, that's all that counts."

And Nicky was so very proud of her.

That evening, as they finished a late meal, too worn out by the stresses of the day to rush or attempt to clean up, Michael tried once more. He wiped the last of the gravy from his plate, ate the bread then looked over. "Can we talk, about anything?"

Nicky sighed before slumping back in his chair. "Anything except the competition or the fool I made of myself."

"You didn't make a fool of yourself. I want—"

"You want," Nicky interrupted firmly. "I always seem to be thinking about what you want, need. Well, right now I can't. Now I have to think of the girls. Like Martha said, it's nothing of your doing. It's our problem, and we'll sort it out. And the other thing? I am not talking about that. So we either try a different subject or sit in silence."

"Is that what you really want?" It was Michael's turn to sound exhausted.

"Yes. So, read any good books lately?"

* * * *

It started slowly, a tiny little thing here, a look or a move there, and it took Nicky days to notice that anything was going on. When he did, slowly becoming conscious that something was happening, he couldn't figure out quite what it was.

Working out why was totally beyond him.

Little things. Little things that, individually, didn't have any meaning or intent. But add them all together and there was something happening.

Michael would sit just that fraction closer on the tiny sofa in the living room, pressed against Nicky from shoulder to knee. He'd pass Nicky the bowl of snacks then rest his hand on Nicky's thigh, the bowl cupped in his palm.

That was at the start, when he was being subtle.

When Nicky didn't register or react, subtle had taken off and flown out of the window, waving goodbye.

Now Michael's hand would be stretched wide over Nicky's leg, fingers flexing, thumb rubbing along the seam of Nicky's sweatpants. Long, strong fingers that he'd watched cutting up vegetables or curled around a water bottle. Watched and thought about.

There were also all the other moments that didn't exactly feel wrong or bad — Nicky didn't even register the meaning behind them — they just felt different from the comfortable, easy way they'd grown together. Maybe there was something in the air, the atmosphere? Maybe he was reading things wrong, because he couldn't say why things were different, just that they were.

He would glance up at odd moments, a feeling, something, prickling along his spine, to catch Michael watching him. Michael's face would be tightly controlled but his eyes would be intent, focused so hard on Nicky that it almost felt like they were burning him. Not in any way that would hurt, there was no nastiness behind the look, just a…a something. Each time it happened, he would ask what was up, but Michael simply shook his head and turned away.

Only it wasn't for long. Less than a minute later Nicky would feel that telltale prickle of Michael's eyes once more.

There were the million and one other things that on their own meant nothing but together…maybe they still meant nothing? Michael would stand too close in the kitchen, offer to rub Nicky's shoulders a little too often and linger a little too long, his hands warm and soothing through the cotton of the T-shirt. And if it felt good, if Nicky wanted to lean back into it? He didn't want to think about that.

Nicky understood actions like those when they were at the gym and both playing a part. He was supposed to be a besotted muppet, after all. That put Michael in the role of indulgent slave who was milking his owner for an easy life. Expected, understood and necessary. But here? In their flat? No, Nicky didn't understand. Michael didn't have to play any role here and he knew it.

At home, Michael could just be Michael, his friend. That's all they were, friends. Nicky constantly reminded himself of that fact.

But even in the dark, in bed, things felt different. Michael would yawn loud and real before rolling closer, till Nicky felt swamped by the heat and aroma of him. It was a heady mix, one that Nicky knew he had to question. He couldn't be taken in by his own reaction to the feel of Michael so close. He had to remember who he was, his integrity. Who they were.

The need for reasoning and order only grew when he woke, deep in the night, to find Michael pushing against his back, Michael's arm hanging limply across his hip.

Now that just plain wasn't fair and he couldn't understand what Michael was trying to achieve. It could just be that he wanted to make Nicky feel awkward after his admission. But what would be the point? And Michael simply wasn't like that—at least, not the Michael he'd come to know. He was straightforward, uncomplicated.

Only now he was playing some kind of game.

Nicky didn't do games. He didn't understand the rules and, more importantly, he hated them with a deep down loathing of anything but honesty.

Michael had some kind of agenda, and Nicky didn't understand it or like it one little bit.

* * * *

As Mrs. Pattinson walked through the gym, Michael bent forward, looking for all the world as though he were about to pick up the chalk packet he'd dropped. But, in doing so, Nicky's hand slid from the small of his back to the warm stripe of naked skin that was revealed. Nicky was pretty sure the move was deliberate. Mrs. Pattinson gave Michael a conspiratorial smile and a warmer one to Nicky.

When he stood, Michael turned his face close to Nicky's and deliberately offered his neck. Nicky had no choice but to put his mouth against Michael's skin, not if he were to look like a true muppet.

He could taste the essence of man, the salt and soap that made up Michael's unique flavor. Could feel the beat of his blood, just under the surface.

This was all so very unfair.

He wanted to…no, he couldn't think about what he wanted to do. For a moment he was lost in the sensations, his head swirling and mind drifting, then he heard Mrs. Pattinson's soft chuckle. "Oh, Nicky," she said. "You're both so sweet."

He could feel the flush creep up the other side of his face, but she moved on before he could hide or process events.

"What did you do that for?" he said, knowing irritation and confusion were competing in his tone.

"Just playing the part." Michael shrugged a shoulder before glancing back to check if the owner was still watching. She was. He grinned intimately, then nuzzled at Nicky's cheek, his ear, his neck, staying much too long, pressing closer than was needed.

"No." Nicky shook his head without being too obvious. "There's something else, something I don't understand. You keep doing stuff like this when there's no need to. You're being—" Then the girls came running into the gym and he had to stop.

"No harm in it, is there?" Michael trailed his hand down from Nicky's shoulder to link their fingers together for a brief moment. He squeezed gently, his thumb stroking over the inside of Nicky's wrist, before letting go and moving away. "I'm just being friendly."

Friendly.

Friendly?

Nicky was left alone and bewildered for a moment before Adeline and Martha came to stand either side of him. Together, the three of them in a row, watched Michael's back as he cleared up—his very broad, inviting back.

"Is he making life difficult for you?" Martha stepped closer, leaning in. "I wouldn't like it if he was, and he seems to have been doing just that since we got back. He's all sorts of fussy around you, flapping and touching and stuff. That's not right, not when it's just us."

Nicky made an odd sound, one even he couldn't interpret.

"I know he's suffered a lot," Adeline said in her soft, appeasing tone, as she also pressed nearer. "But I wouldn't like it either, if he wasn't being kind to you. He should be kind to you, he just should."

"I don't think he's being unkind," Nicky said, trying to defend what he didn't understand. "He's just... I have no idea what he's doing," he admitted.

"You could refuse to feed him or keep him locked up till he tells you," Martha suggested. "That would be a plan."

"Or you could just ask him?" Adeline made it a question rather than a suggestion.

He could just ask Michael. Was that a possibility? Yes, maybe it was. He could ask Michael.

* * * *

That night Nicky cleared up as Michael washed the dishes. They worked easily together, time and habit making the division of tasks simple. No one needed to say anything—they just did what had to be done, anticipating and helping without words.

"There's a movie starting in a couple of minutes," Michael wiped his hands before hooking the tea towel back onto the oven door handle. "One with Brad Pitt and Julia Roberts. We could watch that."

"If you like." Nicky was noncommittal.

"You go put the TV on, I'll make popcorn."

Everything felt normal. If the walls could talk, they'd say it was a familiar scene, one that had been played out a hundred times before. But it felt different to Nicky. There was an air of expectation. A sense that things were happening or about to happen. He thought it was probably the idea Adeline had put into his head. He was going to ask Michael. He'd do it tonight.

But then Michael flopped out on the sofa next to him, mouth already full of popcorn as he pushed at the buttons on the remote control and complained about the TV signal. That was so Michael, so the normal Michael that Nicky had come to know.

Maybe he was seeing things that weren't really there?

Twenty minutes later Nicky was deep into the film and didn't notice as Michael leaned against him, head resting on his shoulder. He hadn't thought anything of it when Michael had turned off the main lights, saying it was easier to watch that way. They often did that, didn't they? He didn't notice when Michael turned his head from the screen, laughing at something that wasn't really funny, till his lips were pressed against Nicky's biceps and Nicky could feel the heat of his breath through the thin fabric of his T-shirt.

But he did notice when Michael's hand went from his own thigh, to Nicky's, then to the inside of his leg. He noticed when Michael's fingers started to explore, when he started to mouth across Nicky's shoulder. He could feel Michael, smell him, sense him through every pore in his body. He noticed when the intent became too obvious to ignore or hide from, his cock hardened, he started to open his thighs then his brain kicked in.

One second he was watching the flickering lights and Julia Robert's flowing hair, the next Nicky was up, off, standing by the wall and turning the lights on. "What the hell?" he demanded.

"What?" Michael looked up from his loose-limbed slouch across the sofa, his tongue dragging across his bottom lip.

"What the fuck are you playing at?"

"Wasn't playing at anything." Michael hitched a shoulder, his eyes dark and hooded. "But we can if you want. I'd like to play, I think you would too."

"Oh no." Nicky stormed. "We are not having that conversation again. I told you no, and I told you why. Is that what you're doing, trying to play me into bed?"

"Not play you, just get you to do what we both want," Michael said seductively.

"So it's all a fucking game? You know I hate games." Resentment crawled under Nicky's skin, making it prickle, making it pulse. "Why would you do that to me?"

Michael sat up, pushing closer toward Nicky in the tiny room, still every bit as provocative as he had been. "Because you won't talk to me about what you said, about loving me."

"I don't want to talk about it, never again," Nicky raged.

"But you won't listen to what I say either, and that means I can't explain it isn't a bad thing, that it can be good for both of us."

"So that's it, you decide we have to talk and I get no choice?"

"But you won't talk, will you?" Michael snorted. "You won't act rational, or be sensible or listen to logic, so I…" He shrugged.

"So you figured you'd play me?" At least he knew what was going on now.

Again Michael shrugged — that simple half hitch of his shoulder and curl of his lip that said so much. "So I figured, if you won't listen, then I'd push things along."

"Push things along? You keep trying to get me all riled up and offering it on a plate, tempting and making it so fucking easy for me to take, even though you know it's not what I want. There I was thinking we are friends," Nicky said, dismissively. "Friends don't do that to each other."

"But you do want it." Michael pushed up from the chair to stand face to face. "You do want it, because you love me, only you've twisted yourself all up, thinking you'd be taking what I don't want to give. I keep trying to tell you that I want it as well, only you won't listen to me, won't hear me when I insist."

"You're only saying that because I made a dumb confession, not because you really want it."

"Balls." Michael spat the word out as he paced closer, thrusting himself into Nicky's space. Nicky desperately wanted to take a step away, but now wasn't the time for backing down.

"Fucking balls, don't tell me I don't want it," Michael snarled again, as he grabbed Nicky's wrist, dragging it forward to press it against his cock. His hard cock. "Does that feel like someone who doesn't want it? I haven't gone this long without getting laid since I started having sex, and you are fucking gorgeous."

"Great." Nicky snatched his hand back, anger and a hint of humiliation filling his head. "So we start fucking because you have blue balls? Way to go in making me feel like a piece of meat or a whore."

"How the hell does both of us getting what we want turn you into a piece of meat?"

"If not a piece of meat then certainly a charity case. You'll do the poor bastard a favor, keep him sweet, and get off as a bonus. It's a win-win for everyone." The scorn was so thick in Nicky's voice you could slice it with a knife.

"But it is a win-win, everyone will be happy."

Suddenly the anger drained out of Nicky as if a plug had been pulled. He stood and stared at Michael. All that glorious, soft hair that he longed to touch. All those acres of beautiful flesh and miles of hard muscle.

That smile, and those eyes and... He wanted. He could admit that, he wanted it all. But it didn't make it right and he wasn't going to be that man. He shook his head, suddenly overwhelmed with sadness. "Except I love you, and you just want to scratch an itch. No, that's really not going to make me happy."

"Don't be like that." Michael reached out again, trying to catch hold of Nicky's arm. But Nicky was already moving away. "Nick," Michael called after him. "We can be..."

"No." Nicky stopped in the hallway. "Right now we can't be anything. I'm tired and I'm..." He sighed, letting the air exhale as slowly as he could, weary of just about everything. "I know everyone thinks I'm a loser but, if I'm forced to play that part then I'd like to be one with a little dignity, even if it is only here at home."

"I don't understand why this is such a big deal," Michael said simply. "You'd never be just a way to scratch an itch. I am really fond of you."

"Please." Nicky made a soft, self-deprecating sound. "Don't make it worse, we have to live together. Give me a chance to get back on an even keel, so we can be easy again."

"What do you want me to do?"

"Nothing." Nicky shook his head. "Go to bed and everything will be fine in the morning. I'll be fine."

"And what are you going to do?"

"Sleep on the floor tonight."

"That's fucking ridiculous, stop being so melodramatic. You go to bed. I'm not going to jump you in your sleep."

"Aren't you?" Nicky said quietly.

"No. I wouldn't," Michael insisted. "I'm not that—"

"I know." Nicky waved him quiet. "I just need a little space, just for tonight."

"Then I'll sleep on the floor."

"No. I'm the one being melodramatic, I'll sleep on the floor." Nicky smiled, a slight curl of the lips born out of a lifetime of being forced into the underdog role.

"But that isn't right, I don't want that."

"Please." Nicky looked up knowing his eyes, his whole face, were oozing vulnerability. "Can we do what I want, just this once?"

Michael huffed, plonking his hands down on his hips as he stared over. "This is insane but..." He shrugged. "If it's what you want."

"It is."

"Just for one night. One night and one night only." Michael wasn't asking, he was telling. Nicky thought about the irony of that as he nodded and went to find the sleeping bag.

* * * *

Martha completed the full pirouette on the top bar then seemed to just hold there for a moment, quite still, quite perfect, her body an impeccable straight line but holding it in a way that appeared effortless, natural. Without seeming to make a move she tipped the hold over to make a giant swing, splitting her legs at the last moment to avoid the lower bar. Gaining speed with another full circle, she pulled up, soaring above the top bar to perform a triple twisting back somersault before landing beautifully.

"Well?" She looked to where Nicky sat crossed-legged on the floor.

"I think we need to put in a more difficult dismount. A full in, back out? You're hitting that well over eighty-five percent of the time now and…hell, I really am an amazingly good coach."

"You're a good coach?" Martha's eyebrow rose.

"Must be. I taught you all you know and you're magnificent." He tried for a grin but still felt a little too awestruck at her routine to hit it properly.

"So you get all the credit?"

"Of course." This time the grin was better. "I get the credit for everything except that hesitation on the toe-on-toe-off move."

"That wasn't a hesitation—that was me protecting my ankle, just like you told me to!" Martha said indignantly.

"Me? I'm sure I never said anything like that. I want perfection at all times."

"But…" Maratha tried again. Just then, Michael came over, resting his hand on Nicky's shoulder, his thumb brushing up the column of Nicky's neck.

"I know my opinion doesn't count for much," Michael said. "But I think that pretty much was perfection. Even better than the fact that every move was smack on was the way you always make it look so effortless. It's like you're floating through the air, so easy and natural."

"Easy takes a lot of work," Martha said, but she took the praise and smiled.

"I know that, as well. I've watched you work, watched you repeat a move over and over, day after day, till I don't think you can stand to do it anymore. But you do and at the end it's…like you were born to do it." Michael stroked down from Nicky's shoulder to cup the back of his neck and played with his hair. It would be so easy for Nicky to lean into it, so simple, to just tip his head and let those strong fingers through his defenses. But it wasn't what he was supposed to be doing.

"Well, I'm glad you think so," Martha said.

"I do." Michael turned his attention to Nicky. "Do you want coffee? Beth just asked me to make some."

"Yeah, sure." Nicky looked up as Michael stroked across his ear, so easy, so natural. So what Nicky wanted but...he pulled his head away, or at least he tried to, but Michael's hands were strong. "Just a hint of milk and no..."

"No sugar," Michael laughed. "I know. Trust me, I know most everything about you." With one last squeeze — as Nicky tensed even more under his palm — he walked away, leaving Nicky and Martha to watch him go.

"Did you ask him what's going on?" she said.

"Yes."

"Did he tell you?"

"Yep."

"Are you going to tell me?"

"Not a chance."

"Thought not," she sniffed. "It hasn't made any difference though, has it? I mean, he hasn't changed."

"No." Nicky sighed. "He hasn't changed at all."

"How about we give up on Adeline's suggestion of asking him and go with my idea of not feeding him or locking him up?"

Again Nicky sighed, deep and heartfelt. "If things carry on like this I might just have to."

Martha patted him on the top of his head. "Take a ten minute break?" He nodded and she gave him an understanding, rueful smile. "I think you're going to need one of Adeline's muffins to get you going again. Only one though."

"You saying I look fat?"

"No." She laughed, brightly and sounding very young. "I'm saying you look kind of pathetic sitting there like that." With that she ran off, and Nicky couldn't even muster the enthusiasm to chase her.

He'd really thought their confrontation the night before would have got through to Michael. He'd certainly made sure he'd kept his distance. First thing that morning everything had seemed fine. Michael had appeared smiling from the bedroom, had passed by Nicky easily on the way to the bathroom — the hand on Nicky's back necessary in the confined space. But then, when Michael had leaned over his shoulder to pinch a piece of toast from Nicky's plate, he'd seemed to sniff Nicky's neck, his nose pressed against flesh.

And that's how things had gone on all morning. A touch here, a look there, a...

Nicky flopped out on his back, arms and legs spread. He had no idea how to handle things anymore. He'd been forced to admit to himself how much he wanted Michael, just how he much he wanted to touch and taste. How attracted to Michael he was. But deep down in his soul he knew it wasn't right and he couldn't go there. Maybe Martha was right — maybe he should stop feeding Michael. He huffed again, feeling every inch the melodramatic princess Michael had accused him of being and went to find cake.

An hour and a half later they were working hard once more. Nicky was with Lily and three other gymnasts on vault, Beth on beam with the others. It was slow going as they were repeating the same thing endlessly. Nicky didn't do shouting, wasn't the type of coach that bullied his gymnasts, but Lily wasn't listening to him.

He took a deep breath and tried again. "No," he said, guiding her back to the vault as she started to walk to the end of the run in. "You aren't planting your hands properly. You have to get the whole of them down, right to the heel. You can't take the move off your fingertips, that isn't right."

"But it feels natural like that," Lily whined.

"It doesn't matter, you won't get enough height to add the extra rotation in if you do that. You have to have a firm plant of both hands."

"But I—"

"Lily," he said firmly. "Do you want to move up to the top rung? Want to be a serious contender in the world all-around competition?" She nodded. "Then you have to listen to me and do as you're told. You need an extra half twist in that vault. You'll only get it—only perform the vault you're already doing right—if you plant your hands firmly."

"But..."

Nicky had had enough. "Go and work with Beth. I'll talk to you later."

"Nicky, I..."

"Go," he said firmly, then turned his back on her. He had other girls who needed his help.

"She'll do what you told her, give her time," Adeline said as she came over from Beth's group. "She just has to think it's her idea."

"I don't want to browbeat her."

Adeline shrugged. "Everyone knows that you know best, even Lily. Where's Michael?"

Nicky swiveled round, looking. Michael was always there somewhere, in the background, doing something. Only this time he wasn't.

"It's just that I heard Mr. Pattinson say that there was a delivery of the big water bottles," Adeline went on. "I don't think Michael should be around for that."

Nicky didn't think so either. A delivery of water bottles meant Willy the driver. Willy was big, amiable, decidedly sweaty and not quite as bright as he should be. He also had a liking for Michael, and he wasn't stupid enough not to know the score.

Nicky gave the room one last glance then sprinted for the corridor. "Thanks," he threw back over his shoulder.

Outside he stopped, aware of everything. All seemed like normal—the smell of perspiration, of work, the sound of feet slapping against the plastic mats, the shouts of praise as a move was performed right, the same snatch of music played over and over. At the end, the backdoor was propped open, watery sunshine filtering in.

If the door was open that meant something was being delivered. He scanned the corridor again. Nothing. No Willy, no Michael, just one of the younger girls running to the toilets. Then he heard Pattinson talking in his office, his posh telephone voice firmly in place. If he was on the phone then he wouldn't have Willy in the room with him.

Maybe Willy was outside with his truck. Nicky started to run toward the open door but his attention was caught half way. Willy's voice, surprisingly high and feminine for a man of his size, laughing, coming from one of the stock rooms.

The door was closed. A bad sign.

Nicky took a deep breath and pushed straight in. Michael stood against the back wall, his palms flat against its surface either side of him, staring straight ahead as Willy ran a hand over his pectoral muscles.

Willy grinned wildly, tongue licking at his lips, drool on his chin, sweat beading on his brow, a manic look in his eyes.

"Hey," Nicky said as jovially as he could manage, pushing past Willy to catch hold of Michael, hand at the back of his neck. "There you are, sweetheart. I wondered where you'd gone. I missed you." He pressed closer to plant a loud smacking kiss on Michael's lips and the smell, the taste, suddenly overwhelmed him. So good. So what he wanted.

Michael, all Michael.

Through sheer will he pulled himself back to the moment. "You know I don't like it when I can't see you." Effectively forcing Willy out of the way, Nicky turned to face him, while slinging one arm over Michael's shoulders and pressing the other palm to his chest. It was a gesture that screamed ownership as loud as Nicky knew how.

He kissed Michael again, this time on the cheek — that was a little easier to handle — then bit at his ear, before glancing over at the other man. "Hi, Willy. How's tricks?"

Willy took a step back, his scowl like a child's. He didn't seem to know how things had changed so fast. "I was talking." Willy nodded with his chin. "To him, to…"

"To my baby." Nicky pulled Michael in tighter. "I know, I saw. Aren't I just the luckiest? I get him and I don't have to share, not with anyone." The implication and tone were clear, even to Willy.

"I weren't doing no harm." Willy pouted.

"I know. Just looking at what you can't have." Nicky reinforced things efficiently then turned the conversation. "How's your mum? Are you still living with her? I bet she needs a good strong man like you to take care of her, especially as she's stuck at home all day."

"She got cable TV installed." Willy's whole face brightened. "We get all the channels now and I can watch when she goes to bed. Have you seen *Futurama*? It's really good."

"I don't think I've caught that one." Nicky put a hand on Willy's back, steering him out of the stockroom, back to his truck. "Isn't that a cartoon?"

"Yeah, but it's not for kids or nothing. It's a proper show, for grown-ups."

"And it's good?" They were half way along the corridor now, Nicky firmly separating the two men, just as firmly holding onto Michael. "Tell me about it."

It was another ten minutes before Willy was driving away, his smile still firmly in place. It had taken every one of those ten minutes for Nicky's heart rate to get back under control. He slammed the back door shut with real satisfaction, twisting the lock into place with even more. He took a deep breath then turned to Michael. "How could you be such a fucking moron? How could you let him get you alone?"

Michael rubbed his hands on the back of his sweat pants. "Willy's not a threat, not really. He's kind of harmless."

"Not a threat?" Nicky's eyebrows hit his hairline. "He would have groped you then turned you around and fucked you good and sweaty."

"I could have..." Michael tailed off but Nicky was in no mood for showing mercy.

"You could have what? Hit him? Told him to fuck off? Either one of those and you'd have ended up back at the slave prep center." He poked Michael in the center of his chest sharply. "I couldn't have protected you. I wouldn't have been able to stop them. What the hell were you thinking?"

"I..." And Michael deflated, the fear showing on his face as he accepted what he'd done. "I sort of forgot, I'm sorry. I won't make that mistake again, not ever. I... Thank you. Thank you, again, for being my knight in shining armor and running to my rescue. I really do appreciate it," he said, honest gratitude in every word.

Nicky huffed, looking back along the empty corridor. "It's not me you have to thank, it's Adeline. She was the one that noticed you were missing." He started back toward the gym.

"Nick." Michael caught his arm, turning him so they could see each other's faces. "Thank you, I really do mean that." Then he kissed Nicky, quickly but firmly on the lips, before he walked away.

Nicky was left with the taste of Michael on his tongue, in his mind, coursing through his body. It made his head spin and his cock harden.

Chapter Six

"How did things go with Lily?" Michael asked from the bathroom as he turned off the shower. "I saw she was acting up today. I've never known Beth to be that angry with anyone."

Nicky tried to remember if he'd locked the front door and pulled out the plug on the old, temperamental TV, as he got ready for bed. "She was okay. She apologized later, then worked her arse off doing exactly what I told her." He turned out the rest of the lights before putting his watch on the dresser and pulling off his sweatpants. "She's a good kid, works hard. She just likes to feel in control sometimes."

"And she's competitive." Michael's voice came through the open door. "She knows the only way she'll be as good as Adeline and Martha is if she listens to you."

"That's because I'm a genius who knows just how to...fucking hell." Nicky stopped, the words slipping from his mouth without his permission as he stared at Michael.

"What?" Michael gave him a mischievous grin, all eyes and dimples.

"I know we have full-sized towels, so why the hell have you only got something the size of a flannel wrapped around your waist? Around half your waist?"

"You don't like it?" The dimples were bigger, deeper. "Want me to take it off?"

"No, I..." Nicky blew out a heated breath. There was all that flesh on show, being offered. Just for him to take. And Michael was offering, no question about it. The way he stood so that his groin was clearly delineated through the thin fabric, the line of his cock drawing Nicky's attention in. Hipbones and cock and a chest that Nicky could revel in, lean against. He dragged his focus back to Michael's face. "You're not going to stop, are you? Not till you get what you want."

"What we want." Michael's voice was low, dark, enticing and inviting, melted chocolate thick and rich, and Nicky wanted. God, how he wanted. Just to touch, to press against him. He could have settled for being Michael's friend. Settled and felt wickedly guilty for the odd stolen glimpse, the accidental touch. But Michael was offering so much more. All Nicky had ever dreamed about having.

He could have it — it was there for the taking. And if it wasn't for the right reasons? Well, he was only human after all.

But what about later, tomorrow?

Michael seemed to read his mind. "This isn't going to spoil anything." Michael took a step closer, the towel only just managing to cling precariously to his waist. "We'll still be friends, still be us. Only we'll be happier, more relaxed."

"I don't want to lose what we have," Nicky whispered, although he had no idea why. "I don't want things to become awkward or difficult."

"They won't." Michael was purring now as he took another step. "It'll be good. We'll be good. Come on, what do you say?" There was only breath and heat between them now. If Nicky reached out a hand, he'd be able to touch, to feel all he'd dreamed about.

"What do I say?" Nicky gave a soft shake of his head, his heart thudding against his ribcage.

"Come on, Nick. Please."

"I'm never going to get someone like you, not here, not for real. Not the way the government has set me up, made me appear to the rest of the country." Nicky looked up, knowing his eyes were dark with want, and Michael would be able to see it. He dragged in a lungful of air and held it for a long, long moment before giving an imperceptible huff as he gave in. "So, okay, you win. I'll take what I can get. I'll sleep with you and be thankful for everything, even if I do know what this really is. I'll be grateful."

"You don't have to be grateful. You just have to let yourself enjoy it." Michael reached out and cupped Nicky's jaw line. "You won't be disappointed."

That first touch was all that Nicky could have hoped for—if he'd ever dared to hope. He'd dreamed and fantasized but never hoped. Now it was here, real, and he melted into the touch, his eyes sliding closed as Michael pulled them that last fraction closer till they were pressed together.

Hard, hard muscle, warm skin and…then Michael was kissing him and everything else was forgotten.

Michael was kissing him.

The first press of lips made Nicky's belly roll and liquefy, and he couldn't stop the whisper of broken sound spilling out. But then Michael moved back, holding his head in one big hand, staring at him hard, a perplexed expression on his face.

Next moment the look was gone, and he pulled Nicky back in. This kiss was quite different — harder, needier, full of purpose and intent.

And it took Nicky's breath away.

Michael's tongue in his mouth, Michael's hand inching its way up under the back of his T-shirt, Michael's knee between his legs pressing up and into him. The hard, hard line of Michael's cock making itself felt against his belly. Nicky had no choice but to give in and hang on for the ride, scrabbling across Michael's back.

Then it hit him like a sledgehammer — that was Michael's naked flesh under his fingers. Naked, still slightly damp from the shower and stretched out under his hands. This time his breath seemed to stick in his chest, making it expand till it hurt.

Michael.

At last.

Then Michael pushed him backwards as he started to explore down the back of Nicky's boxers. "Let's take this to bed." Michael bit at Nicky's lip. And Nicky let himself be maneuvered. *Why not?* If he'd given in he might as well accept all that was on offer. Accept and enjoy it.

Michael gave him a little shove and the next moment Nicky was falling on his back across the mattress, and Michael was staring down at him, heat in his eyes. "Let's get rid of this." He pulled his towel away. Now Nicky really did have something to focus on, something he'd only glimpsed since he'd first been given Michael. Glimpsed — dirty and furtive. Now he could gape with open-mouthed appreciation.

Except Michael wouldn't let him — not for long. After a few moments studying Nicky, Michael knelt on the bed. But the hand Nicky thought was coming up to touch his face never made it. Instead Michael pulled Nicky's T-shirt up over his head, then stroked down his chest. "That's better," Michael murmured. "That's so much better." His hands didn't stop there. Next thing Nicky knew his boxers were unceremoniously grasped and tugged down and off and he was laid out, bare, for Michael's viewing.

"God, so beautiful," Michael said, appreciatively. "I knew you would be. I want this." He crawled over Nicky, kissing his knee, his thigh, the line of his groin, the dip of his belly, then moved up his chest with one long lick of his tongue along Nicky's sternum.

Back to Nicky's mouth, the kisses deep, thorough, demanding and exploring, as he forced his way between Nicky's legs to press their cocks together for the first time. "Want that," he groaned. "Want all of it, all of you."

"What do you want?" Nicky asked. "What now?"

"Want to fuck you, want to suck you down deep, taste you on the back of my throat." He bit at Nicky's throat, little nicks with the promise of more behind them. "What do you want?"

Nicky snorted. "When have you ever taken any notice of what I want?"

"Right now." Michael stared him out. "You want this but you're too decent or too scared to even hint at it, let alone ask for it. So I just took the pressure off you and gave it to you." He pressed their hard, hard cocks together, circling his hips so the pressure was never the same, the pleasure constantly building. "Yeah, you want it." He lapped at Nicky's mouth again and this time Nicky bit back, taking. "But what do you want to do right now?"

"Now?" Nicky dug his fingers deep into Michael's hair, twisting them tight. "Pretty much the same as you. I want to fuck you, suck you. Feel all that skin under me, between my teeth, as I pound into you." He kissed up again, harder, more insistent, forcing his tongue deep into Michael's mouth before pulling away so he could watch him. "I'm not going to get it though. You're going to take what you want first, aren't you?"

Michael forced his hips down so Nicky's legs had no option but to open farther, rising up to rest on Michael's waist. "You say no, and I won't. You have to want it."

"I'd be fucking stupid not to, and I may be many things but I'm no fool." Nicky reached round, grabbed Michael's arse with both hands and pressed it down hard as he could.

"Okay." Michael grinned, wild and wicked. "Later. Next time. Whenever. Right now I have to do this." After one more deep, wet kiss, he was moving, flipping Nicky onto his belly, pushing his way back between his legs, lapping along his spine. "Shit, so good, so gorgeous. This is going to be so good." He slid his palms up Nicky's sides, over his shoulders, pressing, touching everything as he kissed and licked. "So good for both of us."

Then he was moving again, down Nicky's back, fingertips ghosting over his skin, tasting everywhere. At the small of Nicky's back he stopped, rubbing his thumbs in circles as he pressed his whole mouth against the flesh, catching at the fine hairs with his teeth. He stroked, pulling Nicky apart. "Going to lick you open. Going to take my time doing it. Then I'm going to spend even longer lubing you up so I can slide all the way in. All of my cock so deep inside your ass you'll feel me in your belly. Going to spend hours getting you ready to take me, my tongue playing with you. You okay with that?"

Nicky couldn't breathe, couldn't think, couldn't answer.

"Of course you are." Michael licked down the line of his arse—no gentle caress, oh no. This was strong, sure, purposeful. "But you can't ask for it, can't say it, so I'm going to make it easy for you. I'm taking silence as permission. I only stop if you actually say no."

There was as much likelihood of Nicky saying no as there was of him winning the national gymnastics championship—the women's championship.

"Knew you wouldn't let me down," Michael said, then plunged his tongue in, and all Nicky's insides seemed to spasm at the same moment.

Michael pressed against Nicky's hips, holding him down. "You relax and enjoy. But most of all, right now, you need to get used to it because this is only the start. And breathe. Trust me, you're going to need to breathe."

Nicky did his very best on all scores because, true to his word, Michael spent a lifetime getting him ready till Nicky thought he was in danger of going clinically insane. And the sheets were in danger of being twisted between his fingers beyond repair. When the perspiration was fighting for space with the tension between his shoulder blades and his muscles had tightened so hard they were in danger of cramping forever, Michael declared him ready.

"This is going to be so good," Michael whispered against his ear, breath warm and damp. "You and me and...so very, very good." He pressed against Nicky's back, letting him feel his weight, then started to slide in. "You and me and...so good." Michael's voice was huskier still, dark and low, as he pushed and pushed and Nicky thought it was never going to end and he would never fill his lungs again. "So good," Michael said yet again then he was all the way in. "So..." And now he stopped.

Pressure and fullness and the weight of Michael over him, on him. In him.

Through the fog of overwhelming sensation, Nicky could feel Michael's chest against his back, his arms close to his sides. And Michael was shaking, a fine trembling that went through all the flesh Nicky could feel. Precarious, uneven vibrations that stuttered and shook him. "Michael?" Nicky tried to turn his head back, tried to look, but Michael's hair covered what little of his face that Nicky could see.

Michael's breath was harsh and sharp against Nicky's shoulder.

"Are you okay? Are we okay?" Nicky had to ask.

Then Michael sucked in a huge lungful of air, holding it tight for a few moments before blowing it across Nicky's neck as he lifted himself just enough to start to move properly. "Sure we are," he purred. "So fucking good." Next moment he filled Nicky, focusing every thought, every emotion and sensation into what was happening to his body.

Nicky tried to push back into it, but there was no room and no reason. Michael was controlling everything, taking everything. Pushing responses from Nicky's body that he didn't know were possible.

Nicky had been fucked before, not as much as he'd fucked, but more than enough to know how this went. Only he didn't know about this. This was a well of sensations and reactions so deep it might as well have been bottomless. He could feel Michael fucking into him all the way to the tips of his fingers, the echoes of it curling behind his knees, pulsing under his hair.

He didn't know it could be like this. Not with the smell of Michael in his nostrils, the taste of him still dominating his mouth, Michael's sweat on his back, Michael's saliva coating his skin, Michael's cock in his arse.

The idea of Michael in his head.

Nicky gave up and gave in to it, letting Michael take him and take him over. Reveling in the abandonment of control, he felt himself close to the edge without any pressure on his dick. He'd never known that before. He could feel it build, knew Michael could tell as well then...then Michael's hand was on his cock, and he wasn't sure he wanted that. He wanted to let it happen, feel it happen.

But Michael's hand was tightening and tightening, and that wasn't playing fair.

"No." Michael hissed in his ear. "You can't come, not now." His voice sounded ripped, flaking. "I want to suck you, want your spunk on my tongue. I'm going to suck you. You aren't going to come till then."

Nicky was in no condition to argue about it but he thought Michael was wrong. There was no way he could stop, not now.

Only, apparently he could. If Michael squeezed tightly enough.

As each of Michael's thrusts got more erratic, the rhythm more irregular but deeper, his hand gripped Nicky's cock just that little bit more. Not hard enough to hurt, but hard enough to take his attention away from his ass.

He felt it, that moment when Michael seemed to thrust deeper still and his dick pulsed inside him. He felt it again and again as Michael's other arm tightened round his chest, like a steel band, and he pressed his entire face into the curve of Nicky's neck. Felt Michael keep thrusting, fucking into him long after there was any point. Kept fucking while he caught his breath and his twitching muscles calmed.

But he didn't pull out and Nicky couldn't match him in composure till he did. He could still feel it every time his muscles twitched, every time Michael moved even the slightest bit. The thick line of Michael's cock still buried inside him, right inside him. Deep as any cock had ever been. And it drew everything to it — all Nicky's focus, thoughts, concentration. Everything was fixed on Michael's cock in his arse till Nicky thought his brain was going to burst with it.

Only then it was gone, and that was even worse. Just an emptiness that felt bigger, more soul destroying than the fullness. He knew he had to reel himself back in, think rationally and get back a little control, but Michael's big hands were flipping him over, pressing him into the mattress. Then Michael's mouth was on his dick, and he gave up any pretense of thinking, let alone control, and just reveled in the pleasure.

Michael took him deeper than Nicky had ever done or had done to him. He knew that could wreck your throat, and he didn't want any part of that. But Michael wouldn't let him pull back or ease off. He gripped Nicky's hips hard and went to work on his dick. Taking it down so far it must be choking him, pressing his nose into Nicky's pubic hair on the down stroke, sucking on the head till his lips must be swelling on the up.

There was no point hanging onto Michael's hair, he was going to do just whatever he wanted.

Nicky threw his hands out to the sides, stretching his fingers wide, pulling every tendon taut and rode it out. It took pathetically little time before he was coming and coming, emptying himself in a way he couldn't remember ever happening before. Coming while his legs shook, and his neck stretched. Coming while Michael swallowed him down, kept swallowing and sucking even after Nicky had finished, and it was starting to be too much.

Then Michael pulled off, throwing himself over on his back across Nicky's legs, huffing like a steam train.

"Told you it'd be good." Michael looked up at him, something not quite a grin on his lips.

"I'm surprised you can still talk." Nicky had to press his chin onto his chest to see Michael.

"I'll be surprised if you can walk straight tomorrow."

"True." Nicky would give him that. "But you shouldn't do that, shouldn't hurt yourself."

"Never done it quite like that before." Michael rolled over and Nicky couldn't see his face anymore. But he was crawling up Nicky's body so maybe it didn't matter. "Just wanted to this time. Just..." He stopped, pushed the hair from Nicky's forehead and watched him, his face strangely unreadable.

"You okay?" Nicky frowned.

For a long moment Michael just looked at him, then his face lit up. "'Course I am. Who wouldn't be after a fucking like that?"

"And sucking."

"And sucking," Michael agreed. "Shit, you taste good. So good you have to taste it." And Michael moved in, lightning fast, to kiss Nicky.

For a few moments there were flailing limbs and mock fights then Nicky gave in and let Michael kiss him deeply, let the warmth of it spread through his body. He felt sated, satisfied and downright exhausted. This was one night he knew he'd sleep well.

Michael kissed him one more time, lightly and crisply on the lips, then settled down, draping the covers over them both in the same manner he draped himself over Nicky's chest.

"Are you a cuddler?" Nicky asked, as his hand came to rest on Michael's shoulder. "I don't care, I just want to know."

"I like it here." Michael settled himself, his head under Nicky's chin. "I'm comfy."

"Good," Nicky said, mostly to himself. "That's good." He needed to think about what had happened, process events so he could understand and evaluate. Think about meaning and small steps and…the next moment he was fast asleep.

He slept sounder and more peacefully than he had for a long, long time.

* * * *

When he woke in the early hours of the morning, the gray light of dawn just starting to make itself known through the thin gap in the curtains, Michael was wrapped even tighter around him, a leg thrown possessively over his thigh, an arm tight against his chest, Michael's face pressed into his neck so it was in danger of sticking.

Michael.

Michael's leg, Michael's arm, Michael's face. Michael.

He never thought he'd get this, he'd been pushed out for so long and…he stroked his hand slowly, oh so carefully, down Michael's back and said a silent prayer of thankfulness to anyone that was listening, before sliding back into sleep.

He thought he might have surfaced one more time when it was still dark but he couldn't be certain. He had an image of Michael sitting up in bed, staring down at him, watching. But why would he do that?

When he woke again, it was to the alarm going off. Nicky sighed, stretched and felt the pleasing ache in his arse. Last night had been so good and...did they have time for a repeat performance? Not the whole rollercoaster of events, that had taken hours, but they could have a little something, a taste of what was to come tonight.

Tonight. Nicky had every intention of returning the favor and giving Michael the fucking of his life.

He smiled to himself, rolling over to ask Michael if he thought it was possible for them to fit in the shower together. Only Michael wasn't there and the bed was cold when he ran his hand over the sheet. He didn't have time to think about it though because, next moment, Michael stuck his head round the door.

"Morning." Michael was already dressed, ready to go to work. "I made breakfast. It's on the table, help yourself. I moved the alarm back a bit so you could sleep longer, but now you need to get a move on."

"Michael?" He hadn't looked at Nicky once during his well-rehearsed speech. But Michael had let him sleep longer. That had to be good, right? Nicky hauled himself out of bed, muscles and arse complaining all the way, pulled on some boxers and made for the kitchen. Apparently great sex left him starving. As soon as he got there Michael left.

"I'm going to do my teeth, hair and stuff. I'll get out of your way." Still he didn't look at Nicky.

It was the same all the way into the gym. Michael would talk about unimportant things — and Nicky even had to push for that — but he wouldn't even glance in Nicky's direction, wouldn't talk about what had happened. As soon as they arrived at the gym, Nicky turned to him. "Do we have a problem?"

"No. Why should there be a problem?" But Michael already had his back to Nicky and he got out of the car faster than normal. Nicky followed more slowly, stopping to lock the car, stopping again when the door to the gym swung closed in front of him.

"Someone's in a rush," Beth said, coming up behind him. "You two had a fight?"

"I didn't think so. Maybe he's just..." He didn't have an explanation.

"Did you talk to him again about the way he's acting?"

"I tried and..." Then the girls started to arrive, dropped off by anyone prepared to get up that early, the cars barely stopping in the cold morning air. Nicky knew from experience many of the drivers would have their night clothes on under their coats. He raised a hand in acknowledgment as a car horn tooted at him. Then he realized Beth was still waiting for him to finish. "Maybe he'll be better once he's warm and had more coffee?"

"Michael's already had coffee?" She raised an incredulous eyebrow. "Fuck, he must have been bad before it. I don't envy you that."

"He'll be better," he assured her, hoping to hell he was right.

Only, of course, he wasn't.

Michael wouldn't come near him during the whole session, wouldn't even look in his direction. A damned difficult thing to do, given their circumstances. He made sure he was never away from Nicky, never put himself in danger, but his back was always turned. He was also just as careful that he never actually touched Nicky, not even by accident.

With that and an atmosphere you could cut with a very blunt knife, it was no surprise that many of the girls soon realized something was going on. When Nicky called a stop for the day, both Adeline and Martha ignored the rest of the girls as they left. Instead they followed Beth over to him.

Nicky sighed the deepest, most heartfelt sigh he'd ever managed. He might be a bit pathetic at times, but three women telling him what to do was too much.

They stood around him, watching as Michael meticulously tidied up. Way more meticulously than he ever had bothered to before. "I can't decide if it's a good thing that today is Saturday and there's only one training session," Beth said. "On one hand it gives you all afternoon and tomorrow to sort things out with him. But on the other, you're going to have to put up with his bitch face all that time if you can't do it."

"He does remember he's the slave and you're the owner, doesn't he?" Martha asked.

"That's cruel." Adeline admonished her. "He's suffered. Okay, now he's making Nicky suffer and…"

"And everyone else," Martha added.

"And everyone else," Adeline agreed, sounding not quite sure what she was going to say next. "Did you talk to him?"

"I think this is the result of talking to him." Beth laughed.

"So, if this is the result of knowing what his problem is then you have no choice but to lock him in the bathroom and only let him out when you need to pee." Martha folded her arms across her chest in a gesture that was all Nicky's, as she matched him in stance.

"You're serious, aren't you?" Nicky asked her.

"It's that or put up with his bitch face till you get the joy of seeing us again on Monday morning."

"That's it?" Nicky demanded. "That's all I have to look forward to in life? Bitch face and you guys? Someone shoot me now." He rounded on the girls. "Go, now, before I get them to shoot you as well."

"Are you sure you're going to be all right?" Adeline asked softly, after throwing Michael another furtive glance.

"He's not going to ax-murder me in my bed." Nicky snorted.

"Just bitch face you to death," Martha laughed, grabbing hold of Adeline and heading for the changing room.

Then it was just the three of them in the unnaturally quiet gym. "Sure you'll be all right?" Beth asked, no longer laughing. "Do you know what this is about?"

"Yeah," Nicky said, running a hand over his face. "It's my worst prediction come true."

"Do you need me?" She took a step closer. "You know I'm always here if you need me."

"I appreciate that and..." He sighed again. "Can I call you if I need you?"

"Of course you can." She squeezed his arm. "Or just come over to my place, I'm not going anywhere. Any time, just turn up."

"Thanks," he said, and she squeezed his arm again before leaving.

Then there were two of them left—him and Michael. Nicky gave into a bit of self-pity and let out a sigh of epic proportions. "I'm going home," he said at last. "Come, don't come, I don't fucking care."

"Of course I'm coming." Michael glanced up but not at him. "Why wouldn't I come? I have to come, I…"

"Just get in the car." Nicky waved half-heartedly at the group that was coming in to use the gym, then wearily trudged out and across the car park, following meekly behind Michael. He got in, put the key in the ignition but didn't start the car. Only, even he knew this wasn't the place for a heavy conversation or a scene. He was meant to act like an owner, and if he couldn't manage that he could get away with being a muppet. What he couldn't do was get caught having a full on fight with his slave. Slaves had to know their place and if he didn't put Michael there, someone else certainly would.

He started the car and they drove home in silence. Even Miss F's wave and present of homemade — probably rock hard — bread couldn't lift his spirits. When they got inside Michael made to go straight for the bedroom, still not looking at Nicky, as he mumbled something unintelligible.

Nicky had finally had enough.

"Isn't this just fucking lovely," he spat the words at Michael's back. "You promised me nothing would change, that it wouldn't be awkward between us, but what do I get? My worst fucking nightmare of a prediction. I told you we shouldn't fuck exactly because of this but, oh no, you knew better. Well, we still have to live together so we might as well get things out in the open. I'm sorry I was a lousy fuck, sorry you feel dirty the morning after, but I never said I was anything else, never made any promises."

"You're not…" Michael turned round and Nicky caught sight of his face for the first time in a long time.

He seemed completely wrecked.

"What the hell?" Nicky took an instinctive step forward. "Are you sick?"

"No, not sick." Michael pulled at his hair, his face twisting into an ugly grimace. He looked broken, sick with worry, strain or something that Nicky couldn't identify. "Just..."

"What?" Nicky demanded. "Hell, it was a fuck, that's all. So you didn't like it, I didn't live up to your expectations, so fucking what? It doesn't matter. We'll forget it ever happened, go back to the way things were. It isn't that important."

"But it is." Michael stormed forward, only the little table between them. "It is important, so fucking important to me. I've never felt like this before, never wanted to. Only I do now, do want to feel like it. Don't you understand?"

"No, I don't understand a damned thing," Nicky admitted. "You want to feel what? A great fuck?"

"No, don't be so stupid. I can get a great fuck in a lot of places. It was...all I wanted. All I thought I wanted. All I thought it was going to be. But, oh no, you couldn't let it be just that, could you? You couldn't be just a great fuck, you had to go messing with my head, my insides and now everything is all the wrong way around, and screwed up and..." Michael was raving, face red and sweaty, hands outstretched, imploring one moment, twisting together in agony the next.

"Michael, stop it," Nicky all but shouted at him. "What the hell are you talking about? One minute you're rambling about feeling stuff you don't want, the next it's great fucks. So it wasn't a great fuck. It doesn't matter."

"But it was," Michael exclaimed, sounding like a child. "Best fuck of my life."

That was good to hear. Surprising in the circumstances, but damned good to hear. "Best fuck of mine as well, so what's the problem?"

"It's all the other stuff, inside. The feelings and the..." Michael ran out of words, turning a full circle in the middle of the little kitchen.

"The what? What feelings?"

"The love and stuff." It was said as though it was all so straightforward.

This time Nicky's sigh was more a huff of despondency. "I'm sorry. I'm sorry I told you I loved you, but it doesn't matter, we can forget it and just concentrate on the great sex."

"Not you." Michael pulled an affronted face at him. "Are you a total fucking idiot? Me."

"You?" Nicky was losing this conversation. "What about you?"

"It's about me loving. I've never done it before, never wanted to love anyone. Now I want it, I want to grab hold of the feeling and hug it so close that it never gets away. Keep it locked up in a box, in a locked cupboard, in a locked room and never let it see the light of day. I want to love."

"You want to love?"

"Yes. Desperately, pathetically, I want to love with every bit of my heart."

"And the problem is?"

"Just not now, not with you."

And didn't that just hurt like a kick in the teeth. Not that Nicky hadn't heard variations on the theme before. Not usually about loving him, he'd admit that, he never got close enough to anyone for there to be talk of love. But in just about every other area of his life. No one wanted to be friends with the kid with half a red face. They didn't want the loser whose nerve went in competitions working in their gym, just in case that loser mentality rubbed off on other people. Didn't want the guy with the traitor parents living in their block, working close by. Didn't want the man the government didn't trust and despised anywhere near them.

Didn't want to take their only son with them.

Yeah, Nicky knew all about, 'not with you'.

He pulled out a chair and flopped into it, all without being conscious of what he was doing. "I have no idea what to say to you now," he admitted. "No idea how to make this better. You don't want me. I get it. I really do understand. But we're stuck with each other so…?"

"Who said I don't want you?" Michael demanded.

"You did."

"Are you fucking deaf as well as stupid? No I didn't. I said I love you. I just don't want to, of course."

"Of course," Nicky echoed but Michael wasn't listening.

"But no, you had to worm your way under my skin without my even noticing it. I was fond of you, and that was okay, that was acceptable."

Nicky tipped his head to the side, confused beyond words, and watched as Michael marched around the tiny kitchen, arms waving.

"But you crawled your way in, and I didn't know. First hint I get is when I kissed you, and hell, the warning bells went off then. But did I listen? Did I hell. I just went on kissing you, because it was the best damned kiss I'd ever had, and I could feel it in the soles of my feet and…" He stared at Nicky, eyes almost wild. "Don't you understand?"

"No, not really." Nicky shrugged. "Except somehow I infected you, like the Ebola virus."

"What are you talking about?" Michael looked at him as though he was the crazy one, which seemed a bit off. "I'm trying to explain and you're talking crap. I got the first hint when I kissed you, then when I fucked you, it was like I couldn't breathe it was so good, so…" He waved his arms some more. "So right. So meant to be. Like something from a God-damned romance novel."

"And that's bad?"

"Of course it's bad." Michael shook his head, seemingly fed up with stating the obvious. "But still I didn't heed the warnings that were going off so loud I bet half the world heard them. I wouldn't believe what was right in front of me, wouldn't admit it to myself. Such a dumb ass thing to do. But then…" He slapped his hands down on the table, leaning over it into Nicky's space. "Then I have no choice but to admit it to myself because I made the biggest mistake of all."

"Go on," Nicky said, giving up and just wanting to hear the worst. "What did you do?"

"I woke up and watched you sleep."

"That's it? That's your huge mistake?"

"Yes. Don't you see? That's when it hit me so hard I couldn't hide from it anymore, and I had to admit it."

"Admit what?"

"That I love you." Michael stood up again, hands on his hips. "Haven't you been listening, or are you just really, really stupid?"

"I…" Nicky didn't have an answer for that.

"Shit." Michael shook his head in disgust this time. "Right, I'm going to have to spell it out so even you can understand. I love you, and I've never loved anyone before, never wanted to be in love. Only now, it turns out I do. Just not with you."

"You want to be in love, just not with me?"

"Exactly," Michael said, as though that made everything crystal clear.

"No, of course." Nicky sighed. "It couldn't be with me—that would be too easy. People like you don't love people like me."

"Who are 'people like you'?"

"Idiots with half a red face, for a start."

"You're always saying that. You're not an idiot. Why do you always have to be so defeatist all the time? It's like you've given up."

"I haven't given up. I can stand strong when I need to. But life's not exactly been a bowl of success, and you just said I was an idiot." Nicky shrugged. "I've had it ground into me that I'm not exactly God's gift at...anything."

"You're the best fucking coach in the whole wide world."

"Lost it under pressure myself." He shrugged again, dismissively.

"So? Competing wasn't your thing. Your thing is coaching and you're epically good at it. Epically good at getting the girls through the pressure as well. With you on the end of the phone they handled that, it was me that made them lose." Michael loomed over Nicky again, like a teacher telling off a naughty kid. "And you haven't got 'half a red face'. You have a slight blush down one side that makes you look young and sweet, and it's so adorable that I want to lick it half the time." He stopped then, his head tipped to one side. "The other half I want to come on it but that seems kind of seedy, what with the young and cute thing."

Nicky had to think about that as well. "But you still don't want to love me."

"No. Of course not."

"And you wonder why I feel like giving up?" Nicky didn't give him a chance to say anything to that. "Am I allowed to ask why not?"

"Oh come on, man." Michael stared at him, eyes wide.

"No, apparently I'm not allowed to ask. Not an idiot, just not someone you want to fall in love with."

"I can't fall in love with you. Not here, not now."

Nicky looked up imploringly. "Humor the idiot, why not?"

"Because of this fucking awful country. Because you're my owner," Michael said, simply, as though it were all so obvious. "I can't love you."

"I get the awful country part but why not me? Have I ever acted like an owner?" Nicky knew he sounded pathetic but there were times when you just had to know what you'd done wrong. Done wrong this time. "Hell, I've given you everything I have—my home, my food, my money, my protection, even my love and now my body. I have nothing left to give you, you have everything. What does my being your owner matter?"

Michael stopped pacing, turning to face Nicky, deadly serious. Deadly simple. "Because you can never believe me. Never trust what I'm saying to be the truth."

"I..." That floored Nicky. "Why wouldn't I believe you?"

"Because you own me. Because you don't know if I'm lying to make things easier for myself, saying what I think you want to hear."

Nicky stopped the words that were already forming on his lips and really thought about that. Michael had a point. Many, if not all, slaves would say, do, anything to make things easier for themselves if they thought it would make a difference. Michael was no fool and Nicky had made the mistake of telling him he loved him. Yes, maybe he had fantasized about Michael falling to his knees and declaring undying love in return.

But he was no fool either. That was only a dream for three o'clock in the morning when everyone was allowed a bit of poetic license.

Michael's actual reaction was pretty much the best he could have hoped for, knowing the man as he did. He hadn't declared undying love, hadn't looked disgusted at the thought. All right, Nicky hadn't expected to be pressed for sex like he had been, but the rest was right. Michael had said he was fond of him. Nicky believed that because he trusted Michael and knew him.

Now he stared up at the man filling his kitchen so completely. He still believed him, still trusted him.

"Are you telling me you love me?"

"Yes, but..."

"No, no buts. Not now." Nicky held up a hand. "Do you mean it?"

"Yes."

"I believe you."

"Good."

"So there's no problem?"

"Yes, there is."

"Of course there is." Nicky sighed. "There always is. Tell me."

"How are you going to tell if I still love you tomorrow? I can't leave you. We're stuck with each other forever, so I can't ever say I don't love you anymore. You can't trust that I still mean it, and I don't want you thinking it if it isn't true."

"This is what's driven you mad and turned you into a bitch-faced bastard? This?" Nicky asked, incredulous.

Michael nodded.

"Do you know you upset the whole atmosphere and rhythm of the gym today, and that Martha wanted me to lock you in the bathroom and stop feeding you? Even Adeline stopped sticking up for you."

"I'm sorry, I didn't mean to. Martha I get, but Adeline, really?" Michael dropped his head, but only for a moment, then seemed to wave away the idea as inconsequential. "I'm sorry I upset them, but this is important. I can't love you if you can't trust it to be real."

Nicky took a deep breath, thinking. "I promise that if you stop loving me I'll still look after you and protect you. Believe me?"

Michael narrowed his eyes, staring hard at Nicky, then nodded. But for once, he didn't say anything.

"Do you promise, on our friendship, on something that's really, fundamentally important to you, like your mum's life or something, that you'll tell me if, when, you fall out of love with me?"

"I can't make a promise like that."

"Yes you can, I'm telling you to. I need you to."

"I..."

"I'll be really disappointed in you if you don't make it," Nicky said, putting his heart and soul into the words.

It was Michael's moment of truth. He didn't let Nicky down.

"Okay, I promise. But I..."

"No, no buts. That's good." Nicky smiled softly at him. "I believe you love me now, and I'll keep believing it till you tell me otherwise." Then he thought about what he'd said. "Are you really sure, though? I mean, you're a Greek God and I'm —"

"Fucking gorgeous." Michael grinned back at him, but it was far less soft and far more dirty.

"If you say so, but..."

Michael moved closer, stalking his way round the table, pushing it out of the way when there was no more room so he could install himself, standing between Nicky's splayed knees. "Don't let the fuckers running this country get to you. You're worth more than that."

"But I'm..."

"You're the best fucking coach in the world, that's what you are. And you have the most loyal friends. Those girls would do anything for you, so would Beth and Miss F. Plus, and this is a pretty fucking huge plus, you have to be the most decent man I have ever come across."

"Decent?" Nicky raised his eyebrow.

"My God, you never even thought about taking advantage of the situation with me. Hell, it was your right to do anything you could think of. I know how much you didn't want a slave, seemed only fair that you got something out of it but, no, Saint Nicky didn't even consider it. You just spent all your savings feeding me."

"It was the right thing to do, the only thing to do. I'm no saint," Nicky protested.

"I know." Michael pressed in closer, pushing Nicky's thighs obscenely apart. "No one who fucks like you do can be all saint."

"If me and my arse remember right, it was you doing the fucking."

"So it was." Michael was so close now there was nothing but a few layers of fabric and anticipation between them. "That's another thing you've got going for you."

Nicky took the bait. "What?"

"An ass that will keep a man interested for a lifetime."

Nicky thought about the concept. "That's disgusting."

"No it's not, it's...can we stop talking and go to bed now?"

Nicky tipped his head back and looked up and up and up. "Do I get to fuck you?"

"Do you want to?"

"Hell, yes."

"Then I'd say it was a dead certainty." Michael leaned in those last few millimeters and kissed Nicky, a lazy, lust-filled kiss that went on and on till Nicky couldn't think straight. Next moment Michael was pulling at his wrist, dragging him up. "Bedroom. Now."

But Nicky had to stop him, just for a moment. "Are you sure?" he whispered, his breath ghosting over the words. "Are you really, really sure? Because I have to know what this is. I can't let myself think, if it's not..."

Michael caught his face, thumb pressing into his cheekbone, holding him tight. "Do you trust me?"

Nicky nodded.

"Then trust what I say. I love you, just for you. Because of you."

Nicky nodded again, it seemed only right. "Okay. I...want to remember this, want to capture every detail and store it away."

"Why?" Michael brushed across Nicky's cheeks, not tentatively, but firmly commanding. "You'll have tomorrow's memories to replace these, and the next day's and the next and…" He kissed Nicky again, still holding his face.

Michael's hands were so warm and secure that Nicky thought he could lean into them, feel sheltered in them forever. But forever was a long time, longer than he could hold in his mind, let alone consider. Instead he settled for the moment and stopped thinking. He let his eyes drift close and tipped his head back.

"So beautiful," Michael said in an awestruck whisper, right before he kissed him again. "But don't you go all passive on me. You're going to fuck me, remember?"

"Yeah." Nicky opened his eyes as a soft, happy smile curled at his lips. "Yeah, I am. Right now." And this time it was him taking Michael's wrist and leading the way to the bedroom.

The sex was everything he'd never even considered hoping for. Not even when he'd been young and idealistic, thinking that, just maybe, the world could be his oyster. A time before the reality and harshness of life had hit him. Back then he'd dreamed about sex that was more than fucking, but he hadn't really understood what it could mean.

Later, when life had bitten hard, he'd known about the mechanics of sex, the pliability of flesh, but he'd also known about love. He'd seen it unreciprocated in Beth's face, in his own eyes when he stared in the mirror and thought about Michael. He'd seen it when the feeling was mutual and that look was shared. Seen it fade and fall away in many cases, seen it last in fewer, watched it grow and build. What he hadn't known were the implications of the two combined, sex and love. Oh, he'd thought he had, thought he knew about the possibilities and the excitement. But he hadn't.

He had no idea, no expectation that anything could be like this. To look at someone and feel so much, see it reflected in their eyes. See it and believe it. It was there, not so hidden on Michael's face. Not hidden at all. Nicky had no idea that feelings could build and constrict with the touch of flesh on flesh, glance traded for glance, to such an extent that he thought something might just explode. Only to have the tension broken with laughter that seemed to come from his — their — very souls.

He didn't know that sex could be this heady mix of laughter, longing, connection and desire that bordered on the extreme. Sex was about cocks and coming, he knew about that. This...this he didn't think he knew anything about at all, and yet it all came so naturally, so easily. This way of being together.

He was normally quiet during sex — the odd grunt, a short, 'move your arm', was about his limit. It was Michael that had always talked, here, in this bed without sex, where Michael felt safe and protected. But now Nicky felt the urge, no, the need, to say all the things that he normally kept safely locked in his head. That was if he allowed himself to think them at all. Now he could say them because...there was no reason not to.

And Michael encouraged every thought that was spoken out loud with his own words and reactions. His unbridled bark of a laugh when Nicky admonished him for not keeping still as he licked up the inside of Michael's thigh. The way Michael's eyes glittered when Nicky informed him how surprisingly soft the skin was at the nape of his neck. How his face softened and he linked his fingers through Nicky's when Nicky said he liked knowing about Michael's old life, that he felt like he was looking through a window into a golden world.

Michael's whispered, 'tell me how you feel', 'tell me more', when Nicky fought to scratch the surface, so unused to any of this. Unused to feeling, to wanting to put it into words. The meaning behind each touch, the need inspiring each action.

Michael encouraged and added his own words, knowing just when to say something funny, something stupid so they'd be laughing again at some silly thing, at their own absurdity of thinking they were special. Laughing and loving till the urge clawed in Nicky's belly to press his mouth to Michael's skin, to sink deep into him.

"It's okay," Michael assured him, as he pulled Nicky up from pressing kisses into his belly. "There's no rush, but it's time." Michael cradled his head as they kissed till Nicky could stand it no more. Then Michael pulled his legs back and open and it felt so right, so perfect, that Nicky was sure it hurt somewhere deep down in his gut.

As he pushed in, Michael tried to make him go faster, farther, but that wasn't what he wanted. He needed to feel the rightness round him, feel the give of flesh to welcome him in. When Michael pushed up to match his thrusts, he put a firm hand on Michael's hip to hold him in place. "Let me," Nicky whispered. "Just…let me."

"You want it like this." Michael searched his face. "No, you need it," he said with certain knowledge, before going still in compliance, as he tried to temper his own need.

Now Nicky could press in as slowly as he liked, see Michael's shaking belly muscles, the breath stuttering in his chest, his throat swallowing hard. Hear his unsteady gasps, feel Michael's skin under his. Now he could let himself experience it all, rolling and wallowing in every sensation, cataloging them even though he knew Michael had promised him so many more.

There might be more, but there wouldn't be another first time.

As he pushed in the final millimeters, he lifted up on his arms, so that he could lick up Michael's neck to look him in the eyes.

There wouldn't be another first time. This one had to be all he wanted.

"I..." But now, for the first time since they'd made it to the bed, he didn't know what he wanted to say.

Michael did. "I know you love me, and I love you." He drew over the arch of Nicky's eyebrow with his index finger. "And I promise, promise on everything I hold dear, that I'll tell you if I ever fall out of love with you."

Words caught in Nicky's throat, threatening to stifle him. He sucked in a lungful of air through his nose and managed to push out an 'okay' that reflected everything he felt. Then he let everything go and fucked till he couldn't imagine there was anything left in the world but Michael's body and his, and the glorious certainty they were creating.

He'd had sex before. He thought he'd had all he wanted. But he'd never had this.

The idea blindsided him and his arms shook. Michael caught him before he had a chance to fall, wrapping him in a strong embrace, holding him safe as he pressed his face into Michael's neck, open mouth suckered onto the skin.

He fucked in again, hips rolling, glorying in it, then Michael pushed down on his back. Next moment Michael's body was arching under him, the skin over his throat pulled tight as he stretched his head back and he gripped Nicky's arm hard.

He felt the first splash of warmth on his belly from Michael's cock and was left reeling at the thought that Michael had come without a touch to him. Had he caused that reaction? That had made him stutter, his movements losing rhythm and focus. But then Michael's hands were hard on him again, pulling him in.

"Do it," Michael demanded. "Do it so I can feel you, feel you forever."

Forever? You couldn't throw words like that around, but Michael wanted it and... Nicky gave in and gave everything he had. This time when Michael pushed up to meet him stroke for stroke, he didn't try and prevent him. He gave into Michael's hand in his hair, the way Michael wrapped around him so tightly he couldn't breathe, didn't want to. He let Michael's body take over his till he was coming so hard it felt like he was sharing his very soul.

Michael held him securely as it ripped through him, as he fought to catch his breath. After, he lapped at Michael's shoulder and let it all wash over him till he didn't want to think anymore. He just wanted more of this feeling, this contentment. Before he could pull out, Michael hugged him hard, rubbing his face into Nicky's hair. "You," Michael murmured. "Just...you."

Nicky thought he understood. He managed to lift his head up and looked down at Michael. Yeah, he understood all right.

After pulling out, he rolled onto his back but didn't go far, half his body still on Michael's. He glanced over again, scrunching his face up because he didn't know what to say. Michael saved him having to think—saved him and brushed away any tension that might have threatened.

"We are so epic," Michael said seriously. Then his face lit up, and they were laughing again, just like they needed to. Michael bit at Nicky's neck, his shoulder, his nipple, before collapsing back on his side, studying Nicky. "You know, you have the right to expect a bit more from life," he said, serious again.

"I'm not doing so badly." Nicky pulled Michael's arm over another couple of inches, running his fingers up the length, against the hair growth, planting a kiss where he could reach.

"No." Michael pushed at his chest, just emphasizing the point. "I don't mean sex. I mean you should expect to be happy in life, not accept so little."

"I have a lot," Nicky said carefully.

"You might think so, but I know you deserve more."

"More than this?" Nicky made an indistinct gesture to encompass all they were. "Can you get more than this?"

"But you expect so little." Michael snorted, exasperated.

"That's been ground in but I don't let it get to me or change who I am, what I am. They won't force me to be something I'm not."

"You've earned happiness."

"Earned it? I'm not sure about that." Nicky was dismissive. "I don't think anyone earns being happy. But my parents were traitors. I failed as a gymnast when they invested so much in me. I'm…"

"You're loyal, dedicated, kind and have a moral backbone like no one else I know. You deserve the best, you should demand it."

"Demand it?" Nicky's eyebrows rose. "You know it doesn't work like that in this country. I'm damned lucky to have what I've got, to be allowed to work, let alone anything else."

"Lucky? You're the best coach they have. They should be thanking you, not making things difficult. And you should make them."

"Michael." Nicky stroked over Michael's skin again, his fingers soft, his words even more so. "They don't trust me, so I keep my head down and I don't make waves."

"You should have more, you should…"

Nicky pressed his finger against Michael's lips, trying to silence him. "I have more now. I have you."

"And you should have demanded I love you, expected it, because you're so amazing. Not been grateful when I did."

"You can't demand someone love you. You'd never get the right sort of love if you did that, and I don't think any other sort is worth having."

"But you didn't think you were worthy of being loved, that's…."

Again Nicky stopped him talking. "No. I know no one in this country thinks I'm worthy to love, that's not the same thing. And if I couldn't have real love, I didn't want anything else."

"But you should have real love."

"You do though, don't you? You love me." Nicky knew there was a silly smile playing on his face at the wonder of the knowledge.

"Yes, I do." Michael kissed Nicky's fingers, the palm of his hand. "Now you have to get used to that idea."

"Give me time," Nicky said, but it was there, in his eyes, the idea starting to turn into a certainty.

"I'm going to tell you, kiss it into your skin, fuck it into your ass till you know it down to your bones," Michael said as he kissed him, a kiss full of feeling.

And did life get any better than that? Nicky would have to think about it.

* * * *

After spending the rest of the day in bed, Nicky finally fell asleep wrapped once more in Michael's body. He thought he could get used to that very easily.

Late, late into the night he woke once to find Michael propped up on an arm, looking down at him. "Just watching you sleep," Michael said, staring at Nicky's face. "I...I like doing that."

Nicky tried to get his sleep-muddled brain to function so he could say something, but Michael pressed a finger to Nicky's lips.

"I promise you," Michael went on solemnly. "That I will tell you if I ever love you any less than I do right at this moment." He rubbed over Nicky's mouth then bent down to kiss him lightly. "Now go back to sleep."

And Nicky did, just like that.

Chapter Seven

"Can't you turn the music down just a little bit?" Beth bellowed over the rock track that the girls were warming up to as Nicky and Michael walked into the gym. "Please? Just a bit? My brain is bouncing against the inside of my skull. I'm begging here."

The girls ignored her as they went through their complicated dance routine. She sighed and turned toward the door, her face lighting up when she saw them. "Nicky, please, save me. I'm too old for this. You talk them into turning it down, they do everything you say and…" Her attention went from one to the other.

They were standing a clear meter apart, not touching, not even looking at each other, but she picked up on the change, even if she wasn't quite sure what it was. "So you both made it through the weekend alive. I must admit," she said, aiming the words at Nicky, "that I thought you'd have either killed him by now, or yourself. I was hoping you'd still be here, but I wouldn't have laid any bets on it."

"We're both here." Nicky smiled at her.

"So I can see." Again her gaze went between them. "You worked it out and...shit, what have you done? Apart from spend the weekend fucking, because that's like, whoa, written all over the pair of you."

Nicky could feel the blush creep up the side of his face.

"Not the entire time," Michael said, taking a step closer, but not too close. "We stopped to talk, and laugh, and eat and sleep. Only, I'm starving and exhausted so we didn't do much of two of those."

Now Beth's eyes went wide as, yet again, she glanced between them. "But...but...you were being a bastard, and Nicky was about ready to kill you and..." She ran out of words.

"Like you said, we worked things out. Didn't we, Nick?" It was Michael's turn to look at Nicky and no one could miss the way his face softened when he did.

"Yes, we worked it out," Nicky agreed then couldn't think of a single thing to add that wouldn't make him sound like a lovesick moron.

"Oh my." Beth's hand went to her mouth as though she were frightened of letting something out. "You two are...you're...both of you, you're..."

"What?" Michael grinned at her. "What are we?"

"You're all mushy and soft and...glowing. That's it, you're both definitely glowing and it's not just sex that's written all over you, you're both..." Suddenly the indulgent cheerfulness slipped from her face and she caught each one by the arm, turning them round so they were facing the door. "But you can't let anyone see you like that. Fucking shit, there'd be hell to pay, and no one would be safe. It's one thing for you to seem like a muppet, Nicky, everyone gets that. They might laugh at you, but they'd understand it. Only you can't go around looking like you're in love, even if you are. And you." She pulled Michael closer. "You can't stare at him like that, you just can't."

"Like what?" Michael asked, not sounding quite so cocky now.

"Like you want to fall at his feet, like he's the greatest thing since sliced bread, like you love him." Her intake of breath was so sharp it sounded like it hurt. "Hell, you do, don't you? You love him."

"What's not to love?" Michael said softly, trying to look round her at Nicky.

"But you can't, you can't—not and mean it. It's okay for you to pretend, to string your muppet owner along. Some people might not like it, they'll think you need bringing down, but they'll understand that as well. They'll see it as Nicky's fault for being so stupid, so gullible and not keeping you in your place. But you can't mean it, it can't be for real."

"I'm not allowed to love him?"

"No, of course not. You're a slave, you're meant to be fucked and fucked over. You're not supposed to be happy. You can't let anyone see you like this, either of you. You have to pretend. Tell him, Nicky."

"I thought I had, I thought we were already pretending," Nicky said, dejectedly.

"Then you're doing a fucking useless job. Neither of you can act." She dragged them back outside and into the office, shutting the door firmly behind her. Even then she stood with her back pressed to it.

"You can't do this," she tried again. "If I could tell in a glance, other people will get it pretty quickly. You can't put Michael in danger like that. You know that they take away slaves that get too close, take them and sell them. Give you a replacement. Do you want that?"

"No, of course I don't." Nicky ran a hand over his face, up into his hair. Why was nothing ever simple?

He closed his eyes, squeezing them for a moment while he tried to think. "You're right, I know you're right. But we'd talked in the car and I thought I'd, no, we'd, worked it out. That we knew what we had to do. That we have to carry on like nothing has changed. I..." He stopped looking at Beth, knowing he seemed like a lost little boy. "Sorry?"

"You don't have to say sorry to me," she said, gentle now as she rubbed along his arm. "It's nice to see you happy for once. But you do have to be extra specially careful."

"I know, I just..." He stopped, turning to glance at Michael and knew the soft look was back on his face again. This time Nicky could feel it, and he ducked his head to hide.

Michael was just as bad, even if his smile was warmer, dirtier.

"What am I going to do with you two?" Beth said, indulgent laughter coating her words as she shook her head. "Kiss, smile, be happy, draw love hearts on each other's school books but, for goodness sake do it in here. Then come back to the gym acting like normal." Again she stopped, her gaze going from one to the other. "Better still, go back to what you were like Saturday morning. At least Michael didn't look like the happy love bunny on speed. Be miserable—it'll keep you both safer."

"We'll try." Nicky smiled sheepishly at her.

"Try hard," she demanded. "I'm going back. You have three minutes, and then I expect to see you in there looking grumpy, or at least normal. Sort yourselves out, but don't you dare leave any icky stains anywhere in here. I don't want to know about anyone else having sex when I'm not getting any."

"How about if we clear up after?" Michael asked, grinning.

"Shut up," she snapped, then stopped, her hand on the door handle, and turned back. "I am pleased, pleased for you both. The pair of you deserve a bit of happiness. I didn't expect this, didn't think it was possible and I'm going to worry about you endlessly but..." A look full of affection crept over her face. "I really am pleased for you." Then she was gone, closing the door quietly after her.

For a moment Nicky stood there, not quite knowing what to do. "I feel like we ought to have sex, just to prove something to her," he said.

Michael ignored the comment. "Are you happy?" he asked instead.

Nicky thought about it. He'd been happy when the girls had won competitions, when Adeline had brought him cakes. He must have been happy when he was a child — days at the seaside when his parents had stopped reading the newspaper and built sandcastles with him. The morning of his birthday when he first saw his pile of presents. Last Christmas, watching the afternoon film with Miss F, his belly stuffed with food she'd cooked for him, yet another glass of wine in his hand. But he'd never known this, a feeling that went bone-deep, warmed his soul, stirred his belly and left him feeling addicted. He was happy — genuinely, plainly, simply happy. He nodded at Michael. "Are you?"

"I..." Michael also took his time to consider. "I am happier than I ever thought I could be here. I hate that I have to hide it, that it's tempered with being scared all the time, but I'm happier than I thought possible. I never wanted to be in love, I thought it would stop me having fun, having adventures, but now I know it's you, I'm so glad I am." He took a deep breath and his time. "I hate your country, but I love you. You make me happy."

Nicky had no idea what to say to that, and he could feel the cursed blush creep up his face yet again.

"And now I'm too nervous to kiss you." Michael laughed. "Because, if I start, I don't think I'll be able to stop, and when I'm screaming your name, I'm guessing everyone outside will know what's going on."

"You idiot." It was Nicky's turn to shake his head. "Are you going to be able to go out there and act normal?"

"Are you?"

"I'm going to try." Nicky sighed. "The thought that you're in danger will help."

"I'll tell you what." Michael bumped his shoulder. "If you promise I can spend the whole afternoon between your legs, sucking your cock, your balls, licking you inside and out, then I can guarantee I'll be so preoccupied everyone will think I've lost whatever brain cells I had."

"Jesus shit." Nicky hissed. "How am I supposed to act normal after you say that?"

Michael shrugged, his bottom lip caught between his teeth. "I promise you can fuck me. Promise I'll make it worth your while in the most spectacular way you can't ever imagine. Teach you even more new things and won't laugh at you when you're sobbing for more." He bumped against Nicky again as he reached for the door. "If you promise we can go book shopping afterwards, then I'll make dinner as well. Deal?"

Nicky looked at him knowing there was an expression of something like wonder on his face. He'd had sex before—okay, maybe not as great as the sex with Michael, but good sex, memorable sex—he had friends in Miss F, Beth and the girls, but he'd never been in love. Sex with your best friend was like something he'd only glimpsed. Being in love with your best friend, loving them, was something he had never even imagined

Michael gripped the back of Nicky's neck, running his thumb up the tendon. "You're even more beautiful when you're happy." Then he kissed Nicky, wet and sloppy, on the cheek. "Come on. We can do this, even if we have to play-act being real men."

* * * *

At the end of the week Beth lay sprawled out in the vaulting pit with Adeline and Martha, passing a can of diet cherryade backwards and forwards as they watched Michael and Nicky clear up the gym.

"Are they still fighting?" Adeline asked.

"Of course they are," Martha answered her. "They can hardly stand to look at each other and they only bark instructions in the other one's general direction, they don't talk."

"Yes, but...I'm not so sure. I think there's something else."

"When was the last time you saw them touch?" Martha defended her argument. "They don't go near each other unless they absolutely have to."

"You're right." Adeline nodded. "The only time Nicky said anything directly to Michael was to warn him that Willy, the delivery man, was here."

"It must be murder at their place," Martha said, leaning back as Michael and Nicky worked as far away from each other as possible. "I bet the atmosphere is as frosty as a freezer."

"But." Adeline sighed. "Something is different with Nicky and I can't pinpoint what."

"Different how?" Beth asked.

"I don't know, he just seems...softer. But that's ridiculous, I'm not sure what I mean. He's..." She waved a hand around vaguely. "He doesn't look like someone just stole his bike, like he normally does. Plus, I don't need to mother him because he doesn't have that look in his eyes anymore."

"What look?" Beth pressed.

"The one like...like he's outside and can see the party going on inside through the window. Not like he wasn't invited, more that he knows people will talk about him, laugh at him, if he goes in, because he knows how the world sees him."

"Wow, that's complicated," Martha said. "I always think of it as his 'kicked puppy' expression."

Beth couldn't help laughing. She knew what the girls meant, but Adeline wouldn't agree. "No, he isn't a kicked puppy, he's the one left at the dog's shelter. It's a nice home, but all the other puppies got adopted by a family and he was left."

"Oh the poor bastard." Beth laughed louder.

"But he's different now."

"Maybe someone took him home," Beth said.

"It's not nice to laugh at me." Adeline pulled a face at her. "Even if I am silly. But he is different. This morning he actually joined in while we were doing the warm-down dance. Nicky dancing... You have to admit that's different."

"He's happy," Martha said suddenly, sitting up as though she'd shocked herself. "I mean he's often happy, if we do well or do something for him, but this is different, more. Now he's...inside happy."

"Oh." Adeline gasped, as both girls turned to look at him.

"He is, isn't he Beth? Nicky is inside happy," Martha asked.

Beth licked over her bottom lip. "Yes, I think he is," she said carefully.

"He should always look like that. It suits him," Adeline said. Then she turned her big eyes on Beth. "Is it a secret? You know we'll protect him."

"I think that maybe we shouldn't tell anyone else." Again Beth was cautious.

Adeline and Martha shared a smile. "Don't worry, you can depend on us," Martha said confidently, as she lay back.

"Nicky doesn't need us to take care of him anymore, because he's bone deep, inside happy. I like that, I really do," Adeline said, then shrugged. "But I'll look after him anyway."

* * * *

"I'm sorry," Nicky said, licking and lapping across Michael's shoulder to the hollow at the base of his neck—one of his new favorite places.

"Sorry for what?" Michael said, words breathy and needy as he ran his hands down Nicky's back to knead at his arse.

"For putting you in even more danger." Nicky's fingers were, of course, tangled deep in Michael's hair—another of his favorite things—and he used the grip to pull Michael's head back, causing his neck to stretch, his Adam's apple to stand proud for Nicky's mouth.

"How did you put me in more danger?" Michael gripped Nicky's cheek tighter, lifting and pulling at it so he could run his thumb down toward the lube that was still there.

"By loving you. By..." He lifted up, grinning down at Michael as he pushed back toward his thumb. "You said I made you love me and loving me puts you in danger."

"Loving you," Michael whispered, wonder in his voice, "is the best thing that's ever happened to me."

The grin slipped from Nicky's face. "And if it causes the worst thing that's ever happened to you? I couldn't stand that, the thought that I'd..."

Michael pushed his thumb deep inside and Nicky had no option but to stop talking. "It's not your fault I fell in love with you. It's no one's. It's fate, and there's nothing anyone can do about it, it's simply an immutable fact. Now..." He caught hold of Nicky, flipping them over so he was on top. "Stop worrying about things we can't change and let me fuck you again."

Nicky sighed, knowing he sounded just a bit pathetic. "Isn't it my turn to fuck you?"

"Yes, but that's being postponed because you keep worrying and won't let yourself enjoy what we have. How many times have I told you not to do that?" He lifted Nicky's knee high and pushed right in, air catching in his throat as he did.

"Are you going to fuck me into listening to you again?" Nicky asked, hand back in Michael's hair. "I like it when you do that."

"Yeah," Michael said, sighing. "Then I'm going to suck you till you can't think anything else."

"Then I get my turn at fucking you again?" He pulled Michael down to kiss him.

"Soon as you can get it up," Michael promised, as he started to fuck in earnest.

* * * *

Nicky looked up from the box of books he and Michael had bought at the second hand market the day before and surveyed the room. Miss F had fallen asleep in the chair in the corner, like she did after every big meal. Beth and Michael were both slumped on the sofa, feet on the second box of books, arguing amiably about which was the best *Back To The Future* film as the second installment played to itself on the TV.

He could hear the rain pitter-pattering against the window and the wind blowing the litter around outside, but what did he care? He had nowhere to be, there was nothing that he needed to do—if you discounted the dirty dishes still sitting in the kitchen sink. The afternoon would turn into a lazy evening with cozy programs on the TV and the knowledge that tomorrow he would be back in the gym with his girls. Last week there'd been...not a sensational breakthrough in the work, more a coming together of everything he'd been trying to do.

First Martha had tipped and turned her floor routine into something else. She did all the moves with the same precision she always did but this time, this time she'd soared. Not just higher in the air, although she had, but soared with grace and artistry. Something she'd never quite managed before. Maybe it had been the loud, swirling music that had helped. Maybe it was just time, but something magical had happened.

Adeline had watched from the sidelines, hands clasped, her face intent as she watched. When Martha had finished, her hand reaching out with the last notes of the music, Adeline had stayed there, spellbound. Martha had looked first to Nicky and he'd clapped, long and proud, then around to the rest of them. Both Beth and Michael had congratulated her on something special but it was Adeline and her shouted, breathless, 'you were simply beautiful,' that had been the icing on Martha's cake.

When the clapping and praise had finally finished, she'd gone over to Nicky and Adeline. "I felt it," she said. "At last I felt the movements running through me, becoming part of me, just like you two always said. I felt..." She dipped her head, blushing furiously. "I felt beautiful."

"That's because you were," Adeline assured her.

Three days later it was Adeline's turn to bring everything together. Yes, she twisted and flew through the air with her normal elegant style, as though it took no effort. More like a ballet dancer than a gymnast. But she also nailed a complicated Tkachev straight into a Jaeger, two difficult somersaults that, when combined together, were of the highest scoring potential. She did both perfectly, completed the dismount without a whisper of movement and managed to look serene while she did it.

It was Martha's turn to holler and cheer, clapping wildly, while yelling, 'go you, girl'. Nicky gave her a formal bow and declared her a master. Then he gave yet another silent 'thank you' to whatever God was listening that he wouldn't have to judge which of his girls was the best.

Tomorrow he might suggest that Adeline add a twist to one of her somersaults and that Martha put more dance in her beam routine.

But that was for tomorrow. Now was all about enjoying the moment.

He looked around him again and ducked his head, smiling softly to himself. It really was the perfect Sunday afternoon.

"Hey," Beth called, stopping him daydreaming. "You're sitting there with a stupid expression on your face. You're not going soft on us, are you?"

"No, not soft." He threw a pillow at her. "Just..."

"Yeah, I know. You're happy." She threw it back, harder. "You don't have to rub my face in it though, just because I'm still single."

Nicky couldn't stop his gaze going to Michael just for a moment. "You'll find someone and you'll be happy, I know you will."

"Only when Max loses interest in cocks and arse and discovers the wonders of tits," she said ruefully. Then her eyes went wide and she glanced over at Miss F who was, luckily, still asleep.

"She may know more about the wonders of cocks and asses than we think," Michael said. "Her bedroom is under ours."

"Oh God," Nicky groaned, as the others went back to not-watching TV.

He pulled another couple of books from the box, trying to decide where to put them. Middle Eastern cookery and a history of Peru—he really did like books about anything. Then Beth touched his arm gently.

"Don't spoil things by worrying that something will go wrong," she said softly.

"I'm not," he said, and meant it. "I'm going to savor and enjoy every minute."

"Don't think about endings, think about now."

For a moment he caught his breath and held it. "I never expected to get this so I'm not going to waste it with what ifs. I'm going to hold on to everything I have."

"Good." She smiled at him. "Just remember, it doesn't have to end and you deserve this."

They deserved it, Nicky thought. Michael and he deserved their happiness.

* * * *

"No," Nicky demanded, reaching down between them to try to squeeze Michael's cock. "You can't come, not yet. I'm not done."

"Please," Michael begged, pushing into Nicky's body a little more so there would be no way Nicky could stop the inevitable. "Please, please, please, I want to come."

"Not yet. I want you to fuck me more." Nicky went lax under him as he held Michael's hips still for a moment, trying to delay things. "I'm not ready for it to be over."

"Nick, sweetheart." Michael kissed Nicky's neck, his cheek, his eyelid. "We've been in bed practically all day. We've fucked and sucked in every way I can think of till I can't walk straight and won't be able to sit down for a week. Hell, I'm not complaining, but I've licked you from top to tail at least twice."

"But I'm not ready to stop." Nicky pushed his hips up, sliding Michael's cock in slow and gentle. Nowhere near enough to make him come.

"We can start again tomorrow," Michael pointed out, groaning.

"Don't want tomorrow, want now." Nicky pulled Michael's head down and bit at his shoulder before kissing his mouth. "And you've come too many times already, even I know this is the last for tonight. I want to make it count."

"Don't worry, I'll make it count." Michael pushed past the restraint of Nicky's hands. "We don't have time to do anymore anyway. It was your idea to go out tonight."

Nicky's breath hitched, his back rounding as Michael's cock reached deep, deep, deep again. Just the way he liked it. "Not my idea. Mrs. Pattinson's," he hissed through clenched teeth.

"But you said yes to her, that you'd take her." It was Michael's turn to grip Nicky's hips, lifting him so he could work through the slick of lube, hold Nicky open. Pin him as his.

"Can only get away with saying no to the owner of the gym so many times, then you have to give in and put on the fancy suit." Nicky gave up trying to stop the unavoidable and gripped Michael's hair instead. He liked doing that and Michael had a point. Much as Nicky didn't like it, they would have to get up and get dressed very soon.

"But why do I have to go?" Michael got his knees under himself just enough so that he had a base to push from, something to ground himself.

"Because..." Nicky made an inarticulate groaning sound as Michael started their favorite rhythm.

"Forget it," Michael said, squeezing his eyes closed, only to open them again immediately and watch Nicky. "Tell me later. After."

"Just..." Nicky was fighting for breath now, letting it roll and wash over him till there was nothing else but them, joined. Together. "Make it last," he pleaded.

"Anything you want." Michael kissed him again and seemed to try his best to hold something back.

Nicky let his hands run up and down Michael's back, fingers alternating between skimming so he could reach as much flesh as possible, and pressing in so he could feel the muscle underneath. He licked at Michael's shoulder, his neck, chin, lips, wherever he could reach, until Michael picked up the pace and he knew the end was coming. Then Nicky pressed his open mouth to Michael's skin, wrapped his arms around tight as he could, and gloried in the second-hand sensations as Michael's orgasm hit him.

Nicky wanted to feel every moment of it, knowing it was for him, because of him. Wanted to revel in the excitement that he caused before he let himself go.

Michael cried out then sucked on Nicky's shoulder as he rocked through the pulses. As he finished, his hand snaked in between them and Nicky thought he was going to stroke his cock, like Michael so often did to get the added simulation around him as Nicky tensed when he came. But Michael skimmed past to hold Nicky's hip as he pulled out.

"What?" Nicky had to ask.

"You wanted it to last, then I'm going to make it last," Michael said, already sliding down Nicky's body.

Before Nicky had a chance to process anything Michael was already slicking his lips around the tip of Nicky's cock before sliding down, fast and confident. Nicky huffed out a huge breath, stretching his neck back as he dragged in another lungful of air. Michael was just so damned fucking good at this that Nicky didn't stand a chance, already bucking into Michael's mouth.

"Whoa, slow down, partner." Michael grinned up at him. "You can fuck my mouth, but you know how fast you come if you do. If you want it to last, you need me to do the work. What's it to be?"

Nicky tried to say something intelligent and meaningful, but what the hell was he meant to pick? He wanted it all. Instead he groaned, feeble and needy.

"Like that, is it?" Michael laughed, lips slick with spit. "Okay, I'll take pity on you and decide." He rolled onto his back, pulling Nicky up as he went till he was kneeling over Michael's head. "Fuck my mouth, I know how that breaks you apart."

A minute ago Nicky would have sworn he was incapable of holding himself up—now, he was more than ready. Michael held his hips and guided him into a steady, hard rhythm but they both knew it wouldn't last. Within moments he was fucking, ragged but deep, all pace or tempo flown to the wind. He let everything go as Michael encouraged him, and it didn't take long. A handful of thrusts later he was coming, long strands that felt like they were sucked from his core.

Then it was all he could do to roll over onto his back, chest heaving, legs sprawled across Michael's.

Michael pushed himself up on an arm, grinning down with cum-smeared lips. "God, I love you."

"I think you broke me." Nicky sighed.

"I think you broke yourself." Michael laughed. "Man, all I want to do is sleep for a week but we have to get up now if we're going to be ready on time."

"Can't get up."

"Trust me, you really, really need to shower." Michael looked down at himself. "So do I."

"Can't stand up. My legs don't work."

"Come on, old man." Michael grabbed his wrist, dragging him across the bed. "I'll hold you up in the shower."

"Can I lean on you?"

"Only if there's no more groping. Not if we're actually going to make it out the door."

* * * *

Half an hour later Nicky slipped on his jacket and checked his tie in the mirror while simultaneously trying to sort out his hair. "Wow." Michael whistled appreciatively. "You scrub up damned well. I've never seen you in a suit before."

"I feel stupid," Nicky complained. "I want my gym clothes but, oh no, I'm not allowed to wear normal things."

"Of course you're not." Michael stroked over the lapels of Nicky's jacket. "Not at a reception held in the great hall at the Magistrate's Courts. It's classy, so you have to be as well and, I must say, you do a fine job. Want to go back to bed?"

"Yes, please," Nicky said, much too enthusiastically, already pulling at his tie.

"No," Michael insisted. "I was joking, there's no time. You promised to be at Mrs. Pattinson's house in twenty minutes." He straightened Nicky's tie and gave his chest one last appreciative stroke. "I hope she knows just how lucky she is. Lucky that you agreed to go in the first place, let alone looking like this. If I didn't know better I'd worry you were cheating on me."

"What?" Nicky said, incredulous.

"Well." Michael gave a fake shrug of disapproval. "You gave into her badgering, but then it could be

Miss F you're having an affair with. You went down to see her every night this week."

"Miss F is nearly eighty!"

"Mrs. Pattinson isn't."

"She also doesn't have a dick and you do. A really, really nice dick."

"Good, I'm glad you like it. I promise we can do anything you want with it later. That's if you let me blow you while you're still wearing the suit first. You really do look fucking awesome."

"You look pretty good yourself," Nicky said. "I'm sorry you have to wear the slave T-shirt. You'd be amazing in a shirt and tie.

"It's not your fault." Michael shrugged. "But tell me why she wants me to go?"

Nicky pulled a face full of disapproval. "Because she said we were adorable together, even if I was a fool."

"You're sure? It's not just because you don't want to leave me here on my own?"

"No, not this time. She wants you for the same reason she wants me there," Nicky said, looking round for his keys. "So she can walk in with two young, tall men on her arms and watch all the other widows' faces."

"Two young, tall, gorgeous-looking men." Michael kissed him quickly on the lips before turning off the lights as Nicky held the front door open. "Everyone is going to be green with envy."

* * * *

The hall was magnificent, high ceilings, oceans of marble, crystal chandeliers and old, expensive paintings on the walls. The other guests were mostly like the paintings—there was hardly anyone under fifty but the women were all wearing costly jewelry, the men in highly tailored suits. Mrs. Pattinson was a nice lady — she oozed breeding and taste, unlike her son. She was also good company to be around, treating them both respectfully, conscious of why and accommodating when Nicky didn't want to leave Michael alone. She sent them both to collect drinks or food, made sure there was room for them all when she sat down, danced with Michael rather than Nicky.

Even so, they were both only too aware of the looks Michael got. Looks that were now turning into admiring touches and way too many propositions offered to Nicky. He could have made a small fortune if he'd accepted only the first handful.

No matter how thoughtful Mrs. Pattinson was being, they were both feeling the strain. It hurt being this careful, this on show, this tense. "I can't say I'll be sorry to go home," Michael whispered, close to Nicky's ear, as they took shelter in a corner.

Nicky glanced round at all the people still openly watching, then up at the ornate clock on the wall. "Come on." He caught Michael's hand, leading him out of the main hall.

"Where are we going?" Michael followed gratefully behind. "We can't leave yet."

"No, but we can take a break upstairs."

"I didn't think anyone was allowed up there."

Nicky pushed in close, the words only for Michael. "They're not. But everyone will think I'm taking you somewhere private to fuck you. They aren't going to interrupt but they might get envious."

He led the way up staircase after staircase then along one corridor and another, checking doors as he went. "This one will do," Michael said, as they stuck their heads through a door. "It's quiet."

"No." Nicky was sure. "Come on." He kept going, turning down endless passageways till it seemed like they must be at the opposite end of the building, as far away from the other guests as possible. Eventually he found a room he wanted and pulled Michael in, locking the door firmly behind them.

"This is nice." Michael smiled at him, the grin just the right side of devilish. "Are you going to fuck me?" He pulled at his tie till it hung lose. "Or I could fuck you. I bet half the people downstairs would love to watch either way. Although…" Michael stroked his hand over his cock through the thin material, his grin faltering a little. "I'm not sure that after today I can get it up anymore. You wore me out. You might have to fuck me."

"No," Nicky said, just a little wistfully, as he moved to the window, looking out. "I'm not going to fuck you."

"Are you okay?" Michael asked. "You sound kind of, I don't know, sad."

"Not sad." Nicky turned and smiled at him, knowing all the love he felt showed on his face. "I'm glad. Glad I can do this, happy that I have the chance at last."

"Do what?"

"Come here." He pulled Michael over to the window and pointed, his other hand soft on the small of Michael's back. "See that building at the end of this one? The one behind the high fence." He paused for a moment and the atmosphere changed. "That's a garage, one that's inside the American embassy."

"The American embassy?" Michael's voice wobbled on the words.

"Yes." Nicky moved a little closer, running a hand lightly up Michael's back. "Go along the roof here, you'll be able to walk in the guttering, then get over the barbed wire fence any way you can. You'll cut yourself up but it'll be worth it because, if you make it, then you're effectively on American soil." He turned Michael to face him. "You'll be home. You'll be free. Think of it." He caught Michael's arms, holding him tight. "Free." One word that said so much, meant so much. One word that meant everything.

Free.

"Oh God." Michael's voice almost broke as he sagged against Nicky's grip. "Really? There's a chance?"

"Yes." Nicky' tightened his grip, determination in every atom of his body and voice. "But no hanging around, it has to be now."

"Free." Michael tried the word out. "Really free. You're sure?"

Nicky nodded. "I'm sure. Miss F used to work here as a typist, she knew it was the way out. We've been planning it for months but we couldn't think of a way to get into the building, a reason or excuse. Then Mrs. Pattinson mentioned this event and everything fell into place."

"They know, both of them?"

Nicky kept his hold on Michael, brushing arcs against the material of his jacket. "Mrs. Pattinson doesn't. She'd stop us if she knew, but Miss F does."

"That's why you've been going down to see her for the last few nights?"

"I had to be sure of everything—the route to this room, the likely dangers. Everything." His attention never left Michael's face.

"Why didn't you tell me?" Michael demanded, suddenly grabbing Nicky.

Nicky shrugged, giving a soft half smile. "In case it didn't work out, in case you let it slip somehow. It doesn't matter. We're here, we made it. But it has to be right now."

It was Michael's turn to nod as he looked out at the route. "It can be done. Along the roof and then a God almighty leap of faith at the fence and...free." The word stretched out, floating over the quiet in the room. Free.

"Stay low but move fast," Nicky instructed. "Speed is more important than anything. Once we open the window, attention will be drawn up here. It doesn't matter if you get hurt, that can be fixed later. You have to make it over the fence. Have to. This is the only way of doing it and once an attempt is made..." He pulled Michael close so their faces were centimeters apart. "This is a once only chance. Fail and there's no going back to what we had. Prison would be the very best we could hope for."

"We won't fail," Michael assured him. "As soon as you open that window we go. Stay close behind me, so close I can feel you."

"Michael," Nicky said after a long moment, heartbreak leaking through his voice, settling on his face. "I can't go with you. You have to do this alone."

The color seemed to drain from Michael as he tightened his fingers on Nicky's sleeve. Hanging on, desperate and frantic. Disbelieving and unaccepting. "I'm not going without you. I can't."

"Yes you can, you have to," Nicky said, as levelly and calmly as he could. He'd thought about this moment, practiced it over and over. "This is your one and only chance to be free—you're not giving it up. I won't let you. You have to go."

"Then you come with me. We can live in America, you can work there. I know you'll miss your girls but they'll manage, they have Beth. I can't go without you, I love you."

"And I love you." Nicky cupped his hand to the side of Michael's face, pressing with his thumb, stroking it under Michael's eye. Wanting one more touch, wanting it all. "That's why I'll do anything I can to make you free."

"I don't want to be free without you," Michael exclaimed.

"Don't be an idiot," Nicky said kindly. He'd practiced these words as well but it didn't make them any easier to say. "I don't want to lose you but you can't stay here. Sooner or later one of us will make a mistake and someone will get to you. I'll have to go away or you'll open a door you shouldn't or any one of a million other disastrous possibilities. Someone will get to you and hurt you and..." He swallowed, pushing down emotions with the thought. "I can't let you stay when I know there's a chance of you being free. I can't do that and I won't."

"Then come with me," Michael pleaded. "Let's both be free. You can't stay for the girls."

"I'm not," Nicky said, and the heartbreak was back, deeper, more insistent. "I'd come with you if I could, but it's not possible. They won't let me out of the country, won't let me go. If I try then they might come after you as well, and I can't let that happen."

"But you can't be sure, you have to try."

He could see the desperation on Michael's face as he searched around for possibilities. But Nicky had made that journey. There was only one option. "No, I can't because I know they won't let me out. That's one thing I am completely sure of — they won't let anyone go. As a citizen I'd never get out. There are rumors that people have defected but never from inside the country. It doesn't happen."

"But the American government..."

"The American government owes me nothing," Nicky interrupted him. "Why would they risk a major diplomatic incident? Because that's what it would be. My government will not let me go. They'd demand I was handed back and then shoot me in front of the gates of the embassy to make sure everyone gets the message."

"But your government will demand me back and shoot me."

"No." Nicky cut in again, his hand tightening on Michael's face. "They can't demand you back because they've never admitted you're here. They can't say anything at all about you without acknowledging your existence. They won't do that—they'll just cover up any evidence of you. Make it over that fence and you're free. If I come with you then they'd chase us both down with everything they have, whatever the cost." He looked up at Michael, trying to show both determination and honesty in his expression. "You have to go alone."

The hardest thing he'd ever said. The only right thing to say.

"But I can't leave you." Now it was Michael's voice that was laced with heartbreak. "I just...can't."

"And I can't have you stay, knowing I could have got you free," Nicky said simply. "You have to go and I have to beat them. At last, and when it really counts, I'll beat this government and get what I want. I want you free. I win."

"But..." Michael looked about him desperately, as though the answer, any answer, might be hidden somewhere. "But I might not see you again." Then he seemed as though he were about to crumble—a discernible shaking around the edges, instability in his knees.

Nicky sucked in a huge breath, pushing it out through his nose as he caught Michael's face between both hands, holding tight. He had to do this—do it for Michael. "You won't see me again, won't speak to me and I won't ever see you. But I'll know." He shook Michael, his fingers digging in deep. "I'll know you love me just like you'll always, always, know I love you. It'll hurt like a bitch but I'll also know you're free. Free and safe and..." Nicky's voice started to crack, and he had to suck in another breath, clamping down on it while he forced himself from the edge. "I'll know I beat them in the end, that I was stronger than them, and that you're safe. That'll make the hurt bearable." He didn't have a choice but to stop and take yet another breath as Michael grabbed his biceps again.

"I love you," Michael whispered.

Nicky managed a smile. It might have been crooked and watery but it reached his eyes and it was real. "Thank you." The only thing left to say.

"What for? I should be thanking you."

"For showing me what it could be like." He hadn't practiced this but the words came easily. They came from his core. "For giving me so many amazing memories, for making it so that I can carry on. I might not have you but they can't take away what we had. That, the girls and knowing you're free will be enough to get me through. Thank you for being part of my life and making me come alive."

"Thank me?" Michael shook his head, holding on tight to Nicky. "No. Thank you for showing me decency in this fucking awful world, for proving that it can exist among all this filth and evil. Thank you for making me love you." He kissed Nicky hard and needy. "Thank you for being you."

Nicky couldn't hold back, couldn't stop himself clinging onto Michael as he kissed him again, this time desperation overwhelming everything else. He bit at Michael's mouth, pushing his tongue in as far as he could, tasting, touching, his hands buried deep in Michael's hair. Memorizing. Storing it for later.

Then he had no choice but to push Michael away.

"Go, go now," he said, calmer than he thought possible.

"But…"

"Before someone comes." Now that he'd let go, Nicky reached out tentatively, ghosting his fingertips across Michael's cheek. "Before we lose this chance."

"I want…"

"God, so do I." Nicky gave a pitiful attempt at a laugh. "Go. Go fast and, no matter what, get over that fence." He pulled Michael closer to the window, pointing. "Let me see you get free."

"I… You…" Michael's chest was heaving, his hands shaking as he kissed Nicky again, soft this time. Resigned. Then he was reaching for the window fastening.

"Do me one last favor?" Nicky said suddenly.

"Anything."

"Hit me."

"What? No." Michael took a step back.

"Please, make it look like I tried to stop you." Nicky explained. "I don't suppose they'll believe it but…"

"But it might just keep you safe," Michael finished for him.

"Yeah." Nicky forced another smile. "Make it count and make it quick."

Michael stood for a moment, mouth hanging slightly open, his eyes wide and round. The next instant he lunged forward to kiss Nicky then, with no warning, he'd balled his fist, pulled it back and hit him, smack in the face. Nicky reeled backwards, falling over his own feet before landing on the floor.

Michael bent down and kissed Nicky's bloodied mouth one last time. "Always remember," he whispered, close to Nicky's ear. "And thank you."

He turned fast, opened the window and climbed out. "Always," he mouthed at Nicky, as he allowed himself a last look before he was off and running, head bent low.

Nicky sat there for a long moment watching the empty space of the window. He didn't move till he heard the first shouts from below, the first warning shots being fired as bright light suddenly passed across the window, swamping the blackness. He had to get up then, had to.

He had to see if Michael made the fence.

He gripped the sharp edge of the window frame as he leaned out as far as he could. The blood from his nose drip, drip, dripped onto the back of his hands, the lights blinded his eyes, the screams and zip of the bullets hurt his ears as someone started hammering on the door behind him. Then there was a crash and a splintering sound before the room seemed to suddenly fill with people and there were hands on his arms, his neck, his hair, all pulling him backwards.

But they were too late, he saw it. Saw the moment Michael threw himself at the fence, clinging to the top, before he toppled over the other side.

Free.

Michael was free.

That was all that mattered.

Epilogue

"See you later for dinner, girls," Nicky said, as he held the door open for them to pass through.

"Yes, Nicky," Beth, Adeline and Martha chorused.

"And remember, no sitting around going through things again and again," he went on. "You did brilliantly, both of you, and I'm so proud of the two of you." He rested a hand on Martha's head, just for a moment, and she looked up at him, smiling softly.

"I know," she whispered.

"Now, forget all about today and have a nap. Rest is the best thing you can do right now. The second day of apparatus finals are tomorrow."

"Yes, Nicky," they all said again, a little higher pitched this time, a little more sing-song. "We know, Nicky."

"Shut up." He laughed at them. "Sleep's important."

"Yes, Nicky." They did it again.

"You've told us about a million times already. Stop fussing," Adeline added, and she gave him a huge golden smile. She slipped an arm around Martha's shoulders and drew her toward their shared bedroom.

"Come on, let's get away from Mr. Fuss-Pot and celebrate with some chocolate."

"No, no chocolate. Chocolate after the last of the apparatus finals, not before," Nicky shouted after them. "And remember, I'm proud of you."

"We know, Nicky," came the chorus from the girls.

"Oh go away." He waved a hand at them then turned, ready to go up to the floor that had been set aside in the hotel for men.

It was eight months after Michael had got away, eight long, miserable months. At first things had been horrendous — endless protracted interrogations, searches, questioning of Nicky's friends and colleagues. But then, maybe they'd bought his act. He'd tried to camouflage his pain and loss, to make it look like anger at having a slave dupe him. He'd ridden the wave of scorn thrown at him, reveled in the humiliation, because it meant people accepted he hadn't been complicit.

Whether the authorities agreed didn't matter as much as Nicky thought it would. The girls had competitions coming up, they hadn't done well without him and they were the country's best hope for success. As long as the world was laughing at him and he wore his cloak of disgrace, he was left alone to get on with his job. The authorities didn't care about anything but success.

And work helped, it really helped. As did his girls.

He was surprised at just how much all the girls protected him from the shame — even when it was their own parents laughing at him. They protected him and wrapped him in love and care while respecting his pain. They'd come to realize how he really felt about Michael, so they kept working till he was exhausted enough to sleep. They filled his life and his mind with gymnastics and more gymnastics in the hope it would block out everything else. It succeeded a lot of the time. And, as he managed to make it through one day then the next, the girls got even better.

They'd entered a few international competitions but never together. Nicky's rationale was that they both needed experience, but not of competing against each other. He also thought it was a blessing. Adeline had won hers, Martha had done the same. Now it was crunch time.

Now here they were at the World Championships in Rotterdam, and they had no choice but to compete against each other. Adeline had come out in the lead in yesterday's overall competition, with her effortless grace and style, but Martha's skill had put her in second place, a fraction of a point behind. There was only a breath between them and it could have gone either way.

It wasn't a battle Nicky had wanted to watch, let alone take sides on. That morning he'd once again thanked the powers that be that he wasn't a judge.

Today had been a little easier. It was the first of two days of individual apparatus finals. These were competitions that specialist gymnasts reveled in, and his girls weren't expected to win everything. Martha had taken gold on bars, in a display of skill that left everyone gasping.

Tomorrow it was beam and floor. More medals on offer but they already had a gold one each. The pressure was off.

"It's all right." Beth touched his arm. "The worst is over. They'll be okay, we'll all be okay."

"I know but what if..." He pulled a face, not knowing where to start.

"We knew that whoever won the overall competition, the other would be disappointed, that's only to be expected. The girls knew it as well. But it didn't last long," she assured him. "You know how they both work, think. Martha is almost as pleased for Adeline as she would be for herself."

"Almost," he said scathingly.

"Nicky." Beth sounded exasperated. "They both beat everyone else by miles in the overall, there's no one that can touch them. Trust me, our girls know how good they are. They know that the only one that can beat them is the other, and they really do love each other."

"But only one name goes down in the record books."

"You really are determined to make this worse than it is." She stood, hands on hips, and stared at him. "The girls know how it's going to work — one wins this time, the other the next. They know there's nothing but spit between them, have a little faith."

"And if Martha never wins?"

"That's incredibly unlikely, but if it happens then it's destiny and there's fuck all you can do about it. But did you see the way Adeline looked at Martha's bars gold? She may be out sweet little poppet but she'd like that medal. That one is about power and skill. She as envious of that as Martha is for the overall. Those two are going to push each other so they get better and better and better. But at the end, they'll still love each other. Now stop worrying because they know you're proud of them. Hell knows why, but that matters to them almost more than medals."

"Maybe," he admitted.

"Maybe my arse." She smiled. "You do know they don't need you anymore, don't you? I could do your job, but they don't need me either."

"What? No way." Nicky wasn't about to accept that.

"Now they don't need you to win medals. They win them for you. They just want to make you proud." She laughed, reaching over to pinch his cheek. "You've made them so good that they want to win to please their big puppy-coach and to say thank you."

"No, they need me to take care of them. I've got to be there for whoever loses."

"You think?" Beth's eyebrow rose. "They're in their room right now comparing medals. I bet you they wear them to dinner so everyone can see."

"But it's so hard on them. One losing and one winning. It's depressing."

"Oh shut up." She laughed again. "Go and give yourself a good talking to, then we'll meet you back here for dinner. Remember, we won. Two golds, and there's more to come. If you bring our mood down, I will personally kick your butt."

"You kick my butt? You and who's army?" He had no choice but to grin sheepishly back at her. She was right, she was nearly always right.

"See you later," she said. "And remember, no matter what happens, the girls will be fine, because you made them that strong."

He realized she was right as he trudged slowly up the stairs—his girls really were amazing. Letting himself into his tiny attic room, he thought about all the hard work that had gone before. It hadn't been just physical, there'd also been the mental preparation of any top athlete. But he'd gone one step further, building self-worth, compassion and a sense of family.

That's what they were—family. One that took care of each other and wasn't just about self-interest. He knew he'd done well.

As he closed the door behind him, he noticed a single sheet of folded paper on the carpet where it had obviously been pushed underneath. He picked it up, curious. Inside it said simply...

Go for a walk. Turn left out of the front entrance of the hotel and then left again at the first side street. Don't take anything and don't worry about the security policeman, he can go with you. Go now, right now.
M

Nicky's heart felt like it was beating out of his chest as he looked frantically around him, with no idea of what he expected to see. Then he read the note again and another time, just to be sure. He couldn't seem to get his breath, couldn't think straight. But the note had said go now and he knew that handwriting. Knew it in his soul.

He glanced round the room again. He had his jacket and his room key — there was nothing else he needed.

He went back out the way he'd come, stuffing the note deep in his pocket.

Downstairs in the lobby the security policeman stopped him before he reached the door. "Where are you going?" he demanded.

"I heard there's a second hand bookshop not far from here. I wanted to check it out." The lie slipped more easily from his lips than he'd imagined. The policeman had traveled with them and he knew all about Nicky and his love of old books, knew he was a sad bastard and that was all he had left to comfort himself with. "You don't mind coming, do you?" Nicky asked, trying to sound as pathetic as possible.

The huge policeman shrugged. "Why not? I could do with some fresh air," he said, as he followed Nicky out, a hand on his shoulder. Just letting Nicky know who was in charge.

Nicky didn't know what he was meant to do now. Was he supposed to act a certain way? Try and ditch the policeman? Watch out for...for what? He pushed his way through the rush hour crowds, following the instructions in the note to the letter. He went through it again in his mind as he walked, trying desperately not to look as though he were rushing, that he was flustered. That his guts were about to wrap themselves around his throat and choke him to death or the contents of his belly were about to explode out of his mouth and... The note had said go now, right now.

How long ago had it been pushed under his door?

What if he was already too late for...whatever was meant to happen?

He turned left round the corner and kept going. What if there wasn't a bookshop, second hand or otherwise? What if the policeman started asking difficult questions? He ran his fingers over the crumpled page in his pocket, letting the policeman go first as they pushed past the waiting line at the bus stop. What if he made it to the end of this street? Where was he meant to go then? The note hadn't said anything. What if the bastard with the massive dog, standing in the bus queue, wouldn't get out of the way? Then the policeman would get pissed and drag Nicky back to the hotel and whatever was meant to happen wouldn't happen and...

But the dog owner wasn't letting him pass and the rest of the people waiting in line suddenly surrounded the policeman. He was pushing and shouting but he couldn't get to Nicky.

The policeman turned as a big, powerful car pulled up, half on the pavement, right next to Nicky. Nicky could see him try to push his way toward it as the door was flung open, as the man with the dog shoved Nicky closer to it. Everyone knew that the policeman's job was to make sure that Nicky went back to their country in whatever condition was necessary, and the consequences for him if that didn't happen. Nicky knew it, the policeman knew it but Nicky didn't hesitate before he climbed into the car. There wasn't a damned thing the policeman could do about it — not without pulling out his gun and shooting the young woman who had blocked his path with a wheelchair, or the group of school kids, or the nun.

A nun. Nicky was only just awe of the policeman's shouted string of expletives when the man obviously realized he'd been set up. That he was beaten. But that wasn't Nicky's concern.

Nicky was jolted as the car door slammed behind him, as soon as he was inside. The car immediately took off at speed. He gripped the headrest of the seat in front and looked over at Michael's smiling face.

"Still love me as much as I love you?" Michael asked.

"Yes," Nicky said, and he'd never meant anything so much in his life.

About the Author

When Faith was clearing out her attic many years ago, she found a book she'd written as a ten-year-old. On rereading it she realised that it was the love story of two boys. Over the years her fascination with the image of beautiful young men, coiled together as they fell head over heels in love, became a passion for her.

Since that first innocent book—written in purple sparkly pen—she has written many stories, set in varied worlds, but always with two men finding their way to happiness.

Still nothing much has changed because now she can be found in a daydream, wandering around the supermarket, or sitting in a meeting at work still dreaming up stories.

Faith Ashlin loves to hear from readers. You can find her contact information, website details and author profile page at http://www.totallybound.com.

Totally Bound Publishing